Northern Lights Glory

NORTHERN LIGHTS GLORY

(A revision of the original WINTER
HAWK STAR from the Lightning on Ice Series)

Published by coolreading.com, Red Deer, Alberta, Canada.

Managing Editor: Mike Kooman

National Library of Canada Cataloguing in Publication

Brouwer, Sigmund, 1959-

Northern Lights glory / Sigmund Brouwer.

Previously published, Red Deer, Alta. :
Coolreading.com, 2001, under
title: Hitmen challenge.

ISBN 1-55305-044-4

I. Brouwer, Sigmund, 1959- Hitman challenge. II. Title.

PS8553.R68467H58 2003   jC813'.54   C2003-907155-3

We acknowledge the financial support of the Government of Canada
through BPDIP for our publishing activities.

Printed in Canada

CHAMPIONS CREED:

I am a champion.
I will live each day with a passion that's contagious
I will strive to be the hero that I've always looked for
in someone else
I don't need to receive others' recognition to motivate
me:
I play because I love the game, because it reminds me
I'm alive

I will do everything in my power to be prepared
I will train so I'll be ready for practice
I will be teachable and respect those who guide me
I will practice with game-day intensity, each stride,
each shift
I will push and try and get back up
I refuse to cut corners, whine, or put others down
I will not let up, slack, or make someone do my work
for me
I will train on days I don't feel like showing up or no
one else seems to care
I refuse to settle, make excuses, or get sucked into
negative thinking
I will be disciplined, work hard at all times, and make
smart choices
I will take care of the body God has given me & be
thankful for my life
I will be in control of my mind, my words, my actions
I am the same person, whether or not I think someone
is watching
I will take care of the things that I have the power to
change
I will consistently fine-tune the areas in which I have
had success

I will focus on the areas I need it most & will push until I excel

I will risk falling or messing up as I strive to master each skill

I am not afraid to try something new or to face tough challenges

I will wildly celebrate the milestones and enjoy the journey of success

Excellence is defined by what I should do rather than what others may do

I will be a man of character even if everyone else chooses to compromise

I strive to be the best that I can be & to bring out the best in others

I will use my attitude and influence to make a positive difference

I will carry my brothers when they need my help and eagerly serve the team

Success is more about who I am than how I perform, so a winning score only has meaning if I put forth my best effort and can honestly respect myself.

I'm grateful for the ability to play the greatest sport on earth, to face the fear inside me, and to bring my body, my mind, my will into submission

I will bring honor to my family name as I live and play with honor

I will choose to delay immediate gratification in the glorious hopes of winning it all. I am a champion!!!!

Northern Lights Hockey

Hockey Terms

For readers new to hockey, the following definitions may be helpful.

Assist: A player earns an assist by making a pass that is converted into a goal.

Blue line, red line, goal line: The length of the ice is roughly divided into thirds. One third up the ice from each end a blue line crosses the ice. The red line crosses the ice at the halfway point. At each of the far ends, a goal line crosses the ice (see diagram on previous page).

Boards: The entire ice surface is enclosed by waist-high boards that are curved in the corners to match the oval of the rink. A Plexiglas shield above the boards protects the spectators from being hit by a stray puck.

Body check: In hockey, it is legal to run into the person with the puck as long as contact is made with the upper body or hips.

Dryland Training: Players train off ice doing stick handling & shooting drills, conditioning, power exercises, & stretching

Faceoff: A faceoff occurs at the beginning of each period and after each stoppage of play. The referee drops the puck to start play, and the center from each team tries to gain control of the puck.

Forechecker: When a forward or forwards are sent deep into the offensive zone after the puck or puck carrier, they are called forecheckers.

Hat trick: Scoring three goals in one game by a single player.

Hipcheck: A hipcheck is similar to a body check except contact is made as the hip is swung outward.

Icing: An icing penalty is called when a player shoots from behind his blue line and the puck travels all the way across the goal line at the far end. It results in a faceoff in the player's own end, which cancels the advantage of having moved the puck so far.

Neutral zone trap: This is a strategy of sending one man in to forecheck, leaving four skaters in the center ice area.

One-time: The process of hitting the puck without first stopping it.

Overtime: Overtime rules vary in different leagues. In the WHL, it consists of ten minutes of extra play. The first team to score in the extra time wins the game (called sudden-death overtime). In regular season play, a tie at the end of overtime remains a tie. In playoff games, overtime is played until a goal is scored to break the tie.

Period: A regular hockey game consists of sixty minutes of play, divided into three twenty-minute periods.

Point: (1) A single point is given for a goal. (2) In team standings, zero points are accumulated for a loss, one point for a tie, and two points for a win. (3) When a defenseman is standing inside the opposition's blue line, his position is also referred to as "standing at the point."

Power play: Penalties in hockey result in the offending player "serving time" in the penalty box. This time varies according to the penalty. With one and sometimes two fewer players on the ice, the penalized team is at a tremendous disadvantage. The unpenalized team is then considered on the power play. It is also known as a "man advantage" or a "two-man advantage."

Slap shot: A slap shot is the hardest shot in hockey. A player raises his stick above his shoulders before swinging downward to "slap" the shot. Slap shots have been recorded at speeds of well over 100 miles per hour.

Stickhandle: To control the puck by moving it from side to side with the blade of the hockey stick.

Two-on-one, three-on-one, four-on-one, and so on: If there is only one defenseman between the goalie and two attackers with the puck, it is called a "two-on-one"; the other numbers correspond to the various situations.

Roster

NUMBER	NAME	LAST TEAM	DATE of BIRTH	POSITION
2	Luther Deutsch	Inver Grove Heights, MN	7/17/84	F
4	McGrath, Paul	Inver Grove Heights, MN	3/17/85	D
7	Smith, Drew	Rochester, MN	8/09/85	D
8	Sundeen, Blake	Brooklyn Park, MN	11/01/83	F
9	Johnson, Matt	Rosemount, MN	2/09/86	F
10	Larson, Joe	Apple Valley, MN	1/22/87	F
11	Mulholland, Andy	Rochester, MN	5/31/84	F
12	Graham, Trevor	Elk River, MN	7/12/84	F
14	Johnson, Adam	Robbinsdale, MN	7/02/85	F
15	Lokken, TJ	Bloomington, MN	6/02/83	D
16	Almquist, Matt	Grand Rapids, MN	6/29/83	F
17	Kautza, Andy	Merrill, WI	4/03/84	D
18	Bruno, Louie III	Atlanta, GA	2/03/84	F
19	Dobes, Jason	Waterloo, IA	3/13/85	F
20	Hampson, Ryan	Minnetonka, MN	8/25/85	D
21	Jonasson, Jon	Bloomington, MN	6/14/85	F
23	Hogan, Shawn	Apple Valley, MN	11/02/84	F
24	Hanus, Brent	Minnetonka, MN	1/29/85	F
25	Marshall, Ryan	Inver Grove Heights, MN	3/08/85	F
26	Hansen, Tim	Robbinsdale, MN	11/16/84	F
27	Ohmann, Dan	Inver Grove Heights, MN	8/15/85	D
33	Singer, Andy	Lakeville, MN	7/06/84	F
30	Stone, Mike	West Saint Paul, MN	2/04/83	G
32	Kent, Andy	Lakeville, MN	4/21/84	G
35	Johnson, Kevin	Wayzata, MN	1/06/85	G

STAFF:
Eric Fink, Head Coach
Ross D. Smith, General Manager
Rob Talafous, Assistant Coach – Skill Development
Gordie Hampson, Assistant Coach – Power Skating
Ryan Krmpotich, Assistant Coach
Stephanie Smith, Strength & Conditioning Coach, Athletic Trainer

CONTACT INFORMATION:
Email: northernlightshockey@juno.com
8109 Bryant Avenue South, Bloomington, MN 55420
Phone/Fax 952-888-4311

www.northernlightshockey.com

#2

Name: Luther Deutsch

Height: 5'11"

Weight: 180 pounds

Date of Birth: 7/17/84

Hometown:
West Saint Paul, MN

Position: Forward

School: Henry Sibley High School

Favorite Children's Book: *Clifford the Big Red Dog*

Words of Wisdom: Work hard at school –
it will pay off!

Most Memorable Hockey Moment: Scoring two goals
to eliminate Red Wings in the state sectional
playoffs

#4

Name: Paul McGrath

Height: 6'2"

Weight: 205 pounds

Date of Birth: 03/17/85

Hometown:
Inver Grove Heights, MN

Position: Defence

School: Simley High School

Favorite Children's Book: *Yertle the Turtle*

Words of Wisdom: Set goals and work hard to reach them

Most Memorable Hockey Moment: When our team took second at the Minnesota State High School Tournament

Player Profile

#7

Name: Drew Smith

Height: 6'0"

Weight: 170 pounds

Date of Birth: 08/09/85

Hometown: Rochester, MN

Position: Defence

School: Century High School

Favorite Children's Book: *Bernstein Bears*

Words of Wisdom: Never give up!

Most Memorable Hockey Moment: The very first Minnesota WILD Stanley Cup Playoff Game AND being able to see Wayne Gretzky play

Player Profile

#9

Name: Matt Johnson

Height: 6'0"

Weight: 185 pounds

Date of Birth: 11/01/83

Hometown:
Brooklyn Center, MN

Position: Forward

School: Brooklyn Park High School

Favorite Children's Book: *Where the Wild Things Are*

Words of Wisdom: The more you get out of school now, the less you'll have to worry about later

Most Memorable Hockey Moment: Scoring the game-tying goal with 28 seconds left and then the game winning goal with 3 seconds left in the '95 Winnipac tourney (Winnipeg, CAN)

#8

Name: Blake Sundeen

Height: 6'0"

Weight: 200 pounds

Date of Birth: 02/09/86

Hometown: Rosemount, MN

Position: Forward

School: Rosemount High School (Senior, Hockey Captain)

Favorite Children's Book: *There's a Monster at the End of the Book*

Words of Wisdom: If there's a teacher you don't like, don't make it worse by being a jerk

Most Memorable Hockey Moment: At the '03 Stanley Cup Playoffs, watching Richard Parks score on Patrick Roy in Overtime – it was right in front of me!

Player Profile

#10

Name: Joe Larson

Height: 5'9"

Weight: 173 pounds

Date of Birth: 1/22/87

Hometown:
Apple Valley, MN

Position: Forward

School: East View High School (Sophomore)

Favorite Children's Book: *The Wild Things They Are*

Words of Wisdom: Be good to your mother

Most Memorable Hockey Moment: My high school team all went to watch North Dakota and UMN Gophers play at the new Engelstad arena

Player Profile

#11

Name: Andy Mulholland

Height: 5'6"

Weight: 155 pounds

Date of Birth:

Hometown: Rochester, MN

Position: Forward

School: Rochester High School

Favorite Children's Book: *A Big Day at the Circus*

Words of Wisdom: Anything worthwhile never comes easy (including homework!)

Most Memorable Hockey Moment: Laying a check on a player that shattered the glass & put him in the stands

Player Profile

#12

Name: Trevor Graham

Height: 5'9"

Weight: 170 pounds

Date of Birth: 7/12/84

Hometown:
Elk River, MN

Position: Forward

School: Totino Grace High School

Favorite Children's Book: *Bernstein Bears Series*

Words of Wisdom: Use your head

Most Memorable Hockey Moment: Getting the game winning goal to beat the Red Wings in the championship game of the 2002 MN State High School Tournament

#14

Name: Adam Johnson

Height: 5'10"

Weight: 180 pounds

Date of Birth: 07/02/85

Hometown: Robbinsdale, MN

Position: Forward

School: Cooper High School

Favorite Children's Book: *Bernstein Bears*

Words of Wisdom: Stick with it – you'll get it!

Most Memorable Hockey Moment: Watching the Minnesota Wild's first home playoff game

Player Profile

#15

Name: T.J. Lokken

Height: 6'3"

Weight: 200 pounds

Date of Birth: 06/02/83

Hometown: Bloomington, MN

Position: Defence

Favorite Children's Book: *Puss in Boots*

Words of Wisdom: Thank your Grandparents

Most Memorable Hockey Moment: Northern Lights trip to the USA Hockey National Tournament last season and being named league MVP

#16

Name: Matt Almquist

Height: 6'2"

Weight: 195 pounds

Date of Birth: 6/29/83

Hometown: Grand Rapids MN

Position: Forward

School: Grand Rapids High School

Favorite Children's Book: *Mighty Ducks*

Words of Wisdom: I gotta tell ya, work at being honest

Most Memorable Hockey Moment: This whole year with the Northern Lights

Northern Lights Glory

One

When I think of the hockey play that made Riley Judd an instant rookie legend, I always remember it beginning where he's alone against two Ice Hawk defensemen.

After all, most times a forward should not be able to beat even one defenseman. The defensemen have too many options. They can knock the puck away, body check* the forward, block the shot, or move the forward to the side.

Not only was Riley facing two of them alone, but our team was also trying to kill off a penalty. It was late in the game, tied at six goals each. The screaming hometown crowd was going wild. A goal for us would be a huge break. But next to impossible.

And Riley was at center ice, puck on his stick, trying the impossible against those two Ice Hawk defensemen.

1

"Come on, rookie!" It was Brett Beckham yelling, the left defenseman, veteran all-star for the Ice Hawks. The same Brett Beckham that Riley had made look like a fool on an earlier breakaway*. "We're gonna eat your lunch!"

Riley put his head down and pushed the puck up the ice, angling for the opening between the two defensemen. Beckham swung toward his partner, going for a body check that would knock Riley into next week.

At the last second, Riley flipped the puck between them and did a little duck-and-shuffle so complicated I wasn't sure if I had seen it right. It pretzeled one of the defensemen and left Beckham jumping at open air.

Riley squirted through, calmly picked up the puck, and closed the gap between him and the goalie.

Beckham turned and chased Riley, bawling out angry words. "Never again, rookie! Never again!"

Riley paused. It was hardly more than a half-step pause, as if he were considering Beckham's words.

Then Riley put his head down again and broke across the final bit of open ice toward the goalie. Riley pulled the puck into his skates, pretended he was going to push it out again, and yanked it to his backhand instead. The goalie fell for it, sprawling across the left side of the net.

That left Riley the entire right side of the net, with the puck on his backhand, only inches away from the wide-open goal line.

I couldn't believe it. Riley didn't flip the puck into the net to put us ahead. He actually held on to the puck and continued around the Ice Hawks' net.

It stunned the crowd into silence. Riley Judd had just given up a chance at his third goal of the game.

He came out from behind the other side of the net—still with the puck—and skated back toward our goalie.

It was crazy, unexpected. Everybody, I'm sure, was asking the same question that was going through my head: What was Riley Judd doing?

I'd seen a lot from the players' bench before, but nothing like this. Of course, as a fourth-line winger, I see a lot from the bench. A lot of goals. A lot of penalties. A lot of line changes as players step onto the ice. Unfortunately, too few of those line changes include me. What I see most are the backs of the helmets of the guys who get to play while I stay behind on the bench.

Tonight, Riley Judd, playing the center ice position, was one of those guys who stepped past me onto the ice again and again. Only sixteen years old, this was his first game with the Twin Cities Northern Lights. In fact, it was his first game in the Minnesota Junior Hockey League. I knew it. The fans knew it. The media knew it. Everyone knew it. Half the reason the stands were so full was because of Riley Judd, Superstar.

He hadn't disappointed anyone either, not with two goals and an assist* already. Judd's two goals had been real beauties, forcing me to agree with the newspaper articles that labeled him a superstar. He'd definitely shown the crowd he was the Northern Light's new star. All it took was for him to get the puck, and our hometown crowd instantly raised their already deafening volume of yelling and cheering.

Except for now. The silence in the stands was the kind of silence that happens just after a car accident.

What was Riley Judd doing?

He busted hard toward our net, meeting the same two defensemen he had just beaten twenty seconds earlier on his way to their net. Beckham took a swipe at the puck, but Riley skated a wide circle, leaving Beckham to stand

and stare in the same disbelief shared by everyone in the rink.

Riley reached their blue line* on his way out of their end toward ours. He didn't stop. Two Ice Hawks' forwards moved in on him. Riley faked a move left, sprinted to the right, and reached open ice near the center line.

Now Riley was skating in on our defensemen, as if he were a Ice Hawks' forward. Two of the Ice Hawks were chasing him. Everyone else on the ice was moving slowly, staring at Riley, trying to understand.

As he moved toward our blue line and closer to our net, I saw stunned expressions on the faces of each of our defensemen. Were they supposed to try to check their own teammate?

Riley spared them the need to decide. When he reached our blue line, he spun a tight circle, keeping the puck on his stick as if it had been taped to the blade.

At that moment, I understood.

He was going to take another run at their net. Only now, there were five Ice Hawks' skaters between him and their goalie, not just the two defensemen.

Seconds later, as he started up the ice again, the crowd understood the same thing I did.

Their cheers returned in a screaming frenzy.

Riley slowed almost to a stop. He dipsy-doodled in small circles as one forward tried to hit him, then another. With each step Riley took, he kept the puck, dangling it like a yo-yo just out of a baby's reach.

If I had been one of the Ice Hawks on the ice, I would have gone crazy too. They forgot about playing smart positional hockey and moved in on him, wolves pouncing for hamburger.

Riley scooted through the center ice area and came out near their blue line.

Again, it was just him against two defenseman.

"Never again?" Riley asked in a clear yell. "How's now?"

Beckham was so mad he dropped his stick and tried to tackle Riley.

Riley stopped, ducked, and let Beckham rush past him. Beckham tumbled into the other defenseman. As they tried to untangle themselves, Riley carried the puck toward the goalie—his second breakaway of the same shift on the ice.

Against all logic, Riley made the exact same move he had made on the first breakaway. He was so smooth, so good, the goalie had no choice but to fall the same way, backward into the left side of the net.

Riley stopped, backed up, turned his head to watch Beckham charge, then finally slapped the puck into the open net. The crowd erupted into a roar so loud it would have been impossible to hear a jet take off.

Everyone in the rink gave him a standing ovation.

And when he skated back to the bench, Coach Fink suspended him for two games. Riley watched the rest of the game sitting beside me.

Two

As a fourth-line winger, I'm nearly invisible. Sure, Coach Fink knows my name. It's Tyler Watson. He understands my style of play. He knows what to expect from me on the ice. Other than that, I tend to fade into the background. There are twenty four other players who get more ice time because those twenty four better players have bigger roles in making our team win.

I'm not complaining though. It's a thrill for me just to be on the Northern Lights. I mean, someone has to fill in on the fourth line, and it might as well be me. I'm here to train and develop and hopefully get the chance to move up. The other guys can dream about making it from here in the Minnesota Junior Hockey League to Junior A and even playing college hockey. I don't. For now, I just want to be able to put in my shifts without making any mistakes.

I suppose I could be less invisible if I were one of the guys who joked around in the locker room. Or if I could contribute during a really big game. Or if my test scores improved more in dryland and lifting. It's just easier to not be noticed. That way people don't expect things from you. There's no pressure, nothing to fear.

In fact, when Stephanie, our team trainer, stopped in the dressing room after practice and told me that Coach Fink wanted to see me in his office, I began to worry right away.

What could I have done wrong? I'd skated hard in practice. During last night's game against the Ice Hawks, I'd only been on the ice a dozen times. Not enough time to make many mistakes. For that matter, no one had scored on us during any of my shifts. And we won 5-3, thanks to Riley Judd's last goal.

I got out of my hockey equipment quickly, showered as fast as possible and dressed in a hurry. I didn't want to keep Coach Fink waiting.

I left behind the steamy dressing room and the shouting and joke telling of the guys relaxing after practice. I half jogged to Coach Fink's office.

He stood when I knocked on his door. He walked over and greeted me with a handshake. This was not good. He never shook my hand. Was he going to give me bad news? Was he going to tell me they had decided to let me go from the team?

"Tyler," he said, "I've got a favor to ask."

I braced myself. Maybe he was going to ask me to understand his point of view. Maybe he wanted me to find out if I was interested in a trade. "Sure, Coach," I said. "Anything you need."

He looked me straight in the eyes, which meant he was six feet tall, just like me. Of course, we were different in plenty of other ways. His face looked like he was in his late twenties. I was eighteen. He had black hair with just enough speckling to make everyone wonder his real age. I had red hair, cut short because I hate combing it at all. He wore a gray suit. I wore jeans, a T-shirt, leather jacket, and cowboy boots.

"Why don't you sit down," he said, pointing to a chair in the corner of the office.

We played in the Bloomington Ice Garden where the old Vulcans Junior A team played years earlier. Coach Fink kept an office there, which had thick new carpet, wood paneling on the walls, and some art pieces with weird shapes that I couldn't understand.

I moved across the thick carpet and sat in the chair. He was seated behind his desk.

I didn't know where to put my hands. I didn't know where to look. I didn't want to look directly at him and make him think I was being disrespectful. I didn't want to keep staring around at everything in his office and make him think I was rude.

"Tyler," he began, "you study the game. You understand the plays. You work hard."

All of it was true. I hoped, though, he wouldn't add the other stuff about my game. Like I couldn't skate quite as fast as the guys on the first, second, and third lines. That too many of my shots floated toward the goalie like plump marshmallows. Or that when I had the puck I got flustered and never seemed to make a great pass. To me, it seemed like time sped up on the ice, and I never knew quite what to do as the play unfolded around me.

He frowned. "It's like you have all the tools, but you just don't want to use them."

"Sir?"

"I'll tell you the straight goods," he said.

I felt my stomach go into a knot. This was beginning to sound like a bad-news situation.

"Yes?"

"You know the situation in this league with most twenty-year-olds."

I did. Eighteen- and nineteen-year-olds—unless they were superstars like Riley—spent their first years in the league developing their skills and getting their name out. At twenty, any veterans were expected to be team leaders and good, solid players.

"Since day one, Tyler, it's been obvious to this organization that you have potential. In your first year, we thought things didn't go well because you were playing split season with your high school and hadn't quite adjusted to the speed yet or figured out the balance between school and hockey. Last year, we told ourselves that any game you would start to prove yourself, you'd get some confidence, and start doing what we know you can. That game never arrived. We've been waiting and waiting for you to do something, but lately it seems you're happy to just fill a uniform."

Where was this going?

"Well, I—"

" We can't afford to keep rostering a twenty-year-old who doesn't seem to want to go anywhere." He shook his head sadly. "Tyler, we've even put out feelers to see if anyone will take you in a trade so you could get more ice time. No one has been real interested. They've all said the same thing. Tyler Watson doesn't contribute."

"Well, I—"

"You haven't broken our team contract so we aren't cutting you. Our plan is to keep you on the protected roster to train but you won't be in another league game, Tyler. Unless something changes."

Was this good news or bad?

"You've got another month. Maybe six weeks. If you don't start playing like you want to play, we're going to have to give your game spot to someone else who wants to be here."

"I'll do my best," I said. I began to stand.

"Not so fast," Coach Fink said. "There's a string attached. I'm going to ask a favor. It's about Riley Judd."

Coach shook his head. "Here's a kid with as much talent, maybe more talent, than Mario Lemieux. But he's heard that ever since he was six years old. Unlike Lemieux, Judd believes he should be treated like a star."

Now I really wondered where this was going.

"Riley Judd is the best player this league has seen in twenty years. I'll never coach someone this good again. Almost by himself, Judd could hand us the Sommer's Cup Playoff Title. Even with his bad attitude."

Coach managed to grin. "Hey, how many coaches would kill to have this kind of problem?"

I squinted. The question mark must have been all over my face.

"Yes," he said, "a problem. Hockey's a team game. It involves discipline. That stunt he pulled last night was stupid and embarrassed him and the organization. What if this had been a playoff game? What if he hadn't scored? He might be the best player in the world, but I can't let him get away with what he did. It will hurt the team. And, in the long run, it will hurt him. When he hits the Division I hockey scene, he's got to have more than just talent."

Coach Fink paused and tapped his desk with a pencil. "Tyler, you're a lot smarter than you think you are. So tell me, what's my problem?"

"Judd's a million-dollar player. You're not a million-dollar coach."

"Obviously you read the sports section of the Sun Current newspaper today."

"Yes, sir."

"And you heard the fans scream for my blood last night when I refused to let him play for the rest of the game. It's a fine balancing act between keeping fans happy coming back each week and doing what it takes to develop the guys on our roster."

"Yes, sir."

"What this creates is a power struggle. Riley against me," Coach said. "And although my job isn't in jeopardy over this, how I handle him will determine our team attitude and our reputation."

I nodded. Riley Judd was that good.

"Even if I could afford to trade him away," Coach said, "I wouldn't want to. The kid is a joy to watch."

I really, really wondered where this was going and why I was in the coach's office hearing this.

"Fortunately, the owner does agree with me on one thing. If Riley Judd doesn't make an attitude adjustment, it will hurt the team. And it will hurt Riley Judd. He's got to learn the world doesn't revolve around him just because he's a star hockey player."

"Coach?"

"This year, the Board of Directors have gotten us involved with a group called New Hope. It's an inner-city organization that helps kids from disadvantaged backgrounds." Coach Fink shrugged. "Our General Manager knows someone on the board of directors of Youth Works. One night they had dinner together and came up with the idea to send a couple of players from the team to help the kids as one of our official team community service projects."

Coach Fink pointed at me. "You're one of the players. Riley will be the other. I know that you already completed your 100 hours of service to fulfill your contract, so this is above what we ask players to commit to do. But maybe that way Riley will learn something about real life. You're both going into the inner city to do some volunteer work on behalf of the Northern Lights."

"Me, sir?" This didn't sound like I was volunteering.

"Look, Tyler. You're a sensible kid. That's why I'm explaining all this to you. Which, by the way, you're not going to repeat to Riley Judd. Right?"

"Right, sir."

"Your job is to make sure he actually spends time with the kids. We'll even reimburse you gas money for driving him there and back. Your job is to make sure he doesn't get in trouble. Your job is to be a good influence on Riley Judd."

"Yes, sir."

"You'll spend four hours a week at the organization. Every Tuesday and Thursday afternoon, you and Riley will represent the Northern Lights and spend time with the kids, doing whatever the people there see fit."

"But, I—"

"Do you want six weeks to prove that you are willing to serve the team and be part of the bigger picture? Are you willing to help bring out the potential in a teammate by helping him get his act together? Or do you want to sit during game time for awhile to figure it out? That's the same choice I offered Riley. Well?"

He stared at me, waiting for my answer.

"What time did you want us there, Coach?" I asked. "And what's the address?"

Three

"I don't have to do this," Riley Judd told me.

I was looking for street signs as I drove, so I ignored him. Besides, he'd been saying that since he got in my Jeep Cherokee a half hour earlier. He was saying it just to get me to argue with him. The truth was, he really did have to do this. Part of the contract that we sign as Northern Lights players states that we will make ourselves available for public functions as members of the team.

"Minnehaha," I said. "We're getting closer. Coach told us to quickly get in the right lane and watch sign."

"Minnehaha. All of this sounds dumb."

"Look there's the turn off we took to get to Lake Minnehaha park with the waterfall." I pointed, "Lake Street exit. See?"

Riley quit grumbling long enough to look.

"Cool," Riley said, although by the tone of his voice he meant otherwise. "First, you're a taxi driver. Now a tour guide?"

I nearly told him I felt like a baby-sitter, but I managed to keep my mouth shut.

It was four o'clock, so afternoon traffic was heavy. Finally we reached the Lake Street exit where I turned right and quickly made a left on 5th Avenue. We drove another few minutes. It didn't take long before the buildings we were passing began to look run down. There were a few vacant lots, old houses in poor repair, and graffiti covered the bridges. There were a few newly renovated projects and a mini soccer field, but it didn't look like the plush Minnetonka suburbs where I lived with my host family.

We passed a man in a big brown overcoat. He was pushing a shopping cart filled with empty bottles.

"Nice neighborhood," Riley said, again not meaning what he said.

"The kids we're visiting have to grow up in this area."

"They should have been smart enough to be born into different families."

What a jerk. I slammed on the brakes. It

snapped Riley ahead into his seat belt.

"Hey! Why'd you do that?"

"We're here," I said. "New Hope Mission."

Just as Coach Fink had promised, the building had been easy to find. All I had to do was keep my eyes open for the three story house with the big cross. I'd heard that the Baptist convention had purchased the building for weekly worship services and to start a mission working primarily with children from the neighborhood. The church building was set back from the street. I was willing to bet it was at least a hundred years old.

In fading letters on a dirty white background, the sign stuck crookedly into the ground read: HOME TO NEW HOPE.

The lawn between the sidewalk and the church was worn down, almost lumpy. I could guess why. About twenty kids were playing soccer in the yard the rest of the group were playing basketball. They were running and screaming and doing all the things kids do when you let them loose outside.

"We might as well get started," I said. "We're supposed to ask for someone named Sam."

"Probably some dry, dusty old janitor type," Riley said. "I think I'll wait in the car."

"Suit yourself."

"I always do," Riley said. "In fact, I think I'll

just wait in the car for the entire two hours. Tell me what it was like when you get back."

"Suit yourself."

I left him there and crossed the hard ground of the lawn. The kids ignored me. They had more important things on their minds. Like yelling and screaming and chasing each other.

I managed to make it across without stepping on any of them. I knocked on a set of doors at the side of the church building. Within thirty seconds, the door swung open.

I found it hard to speak. I almost found it hard to breathe. A girl who looks like she just stepped out of a magazine ad will do that to a guy.

She wore blue jeans and a white T-shirt. She had long dark hair that hung in loose curls. She had deep brown eyes. She had a slow, wide smile. She had me in the palm of her hand.

"Hello?" she said. It might have been her second or third hello. I was still trying to find air to speak.

"Um," I said.

She laughed. "That's a good start. Are you from the Northern Lights?"

"Um," I said.

"I can guess by your jacket."

I looked down. Of course. My team jacket. The

one with Northern Lights written in big letters.

"Um," I said.

"We've been expecting you," she said. Her smile became a slight frown. "But I thought there would be two of you."

"Um," I said.

"Oh, there he is." She looked past me, at my car. I looked with her. Riley was jogging across the grass toward us with a big grin on his face. He neatly sidestepped a couple of kids, as if he were a football player on his way to a touchdown.

"Um," I said.

Riley slapped me on the back as he joined us.

"Hey, bud," he said. "Next time wait for me to get my shoes tied, will you?"

He turned his grin toward the girl in the doorway. Riley is nearly my height. He has dark hair and blue eyes and a dimple in the center of his chin. He fills his Northern Lights jacket like he's lifted weights since he was ten years old, which, of course, he has. He has a strut that shows he's afraid of no one. With my short red hair and too many freckles on a face with no dimples and no wonderful smile, I was just a mutt wagging his tail beside a show dog.

"The name's Riley Judd," he said to the girl. He stuck his hand out for her to shake, which she did. With a nice big smile for him.

"I've been looking forward to helping out with the kids. In a neighborhood like this, they need as many breaks as they can get." Riley shook his head sadly in sympathy for them. "The big guy here hasn't been so keen, but we'll work on him, right?"

She laughed. Riley was still holding her hand. "Right," she said. "We'll work on him."

The screams of laughter on the lawn rose and fell as they continued to hold hands and look at each other.

Riley finally let go of her hand. "Well," he said, "the first thing we need to do is talk to someone named Sam. Any chance you can help us?"

"I'm Sam," she said. "I'm in charge of the after school programs here."

"You're Sam?" Riley asked. "You don't look like a Sam."

"Um," I said.

"Actually, I'm Samantha. Samantha Blair."

"Sam for short," Riley said. "I like that. It's kind of classy."

She rewarded him with another smile.

"You don't look much older than us," Riley said.

"I'm eighteen. I skipped a grade in elementary school. Graduated high school early. I'm taking a semester off to work with the kids before I go to college."

"Um," I said. Why could Riley find things to say, and why did my tongue feel like a block of wood?

"It's great that you guys could help," she said. "Mostly, we just want you to spend time with the kids. A lot of them come from broken homes. New Hope is a place where they don't have to worry about getting beat up by parents or gang members. When school finishes for the day, they come here instead of going home. We try to make sure they get exercise, good food, and a friendly ear to listen to their problems. We—"

She stopped herself and shot a startled glance over our shoulders.

"That's my brother, Ben! What are they doing with him?"

We followed her gaze. Two white men were standing in the middle of a bunch of kids. They had grabbed a seven- or eight-year-old kid by his arms and were dragging him toward the open side door of a blue van parked in front of my Jeep.

From the ski masks over their faces, it was easy to guess they weren't Ben's friends.

Four

They threw Ben into the van. One of the men jumped in behind him and slid the door shut. The other man ran around the front of the van and jumped behind the steering wheel.

"You drove, right?" Samantha asked.

I nodded. The keys to my Jeep were still dangling in my hand.

She grabbed my wrist and started dragging me toward the street. I stumbled after her. The kids on the lawn were all frozen in shock, quiet and staring in the direction of the disappearing van.

"What about me?" Riley shouted.

"Call the police!" she shouted over her shoulder. "Tell them what happened!"

I had to run to keep up with her. The kids made room for us as we passed through the group.

I sprinted past her, cutting around the front of the Jeep and sliding in behind the steering wheel as she managed to get in the passenger side.

The Jeep started with a roar. I gunned it, and we jumped ahead.

"Seat belt!" I shouted. I scrambled to get mine on before we squealed around the first corner.

The van was a block away.

I pressed the gas pedal to the floor. We closed the gap to half a block.

"License plates," I told her. Time seemed to be like a slow current. I felt strangely calm and clearheaded. "Get the number. There's pen and paper in the glove box."

She scrambled to find the paper. I concentrated on the road.

Now the van was a quarter block away. Close enough to see the plates. Close enough to see we wouldn't get the number.

Samantha slammed the dash with her fist in frustration. The back end of the blue van was covered with mud, and the van's license plates were impossible to see.

At that moment, the van driver must have realized we were chasing him. A huge cloud of black smoke mushroomed from the van's exhaust pipe, and it started to slip away.

I glanced at my speedometer. Fifty miles an hour. I thought of the rush-hour traffic on the main roads. He'd be forced to slow down as soon as we got off these side streets.

Brake lights suddenly showed on the van. It skidded sideways to make a right turn at the next intersection.

I slammed on my own brakes and wrestled with the steering wheel to keep from sliding out of control. I turned hard to make the corner.

The van had turned maybe five seconds before we reached the intersection. And five seconds earlier, both lanes had been clear. The van had been able to skid through the far lane, then veer back onto the right side of the road.

Not us. In those five seconds, a small truck had almost reached the stop sign of the cross street. And we were also skidding into the far lane, a half second away from slamming into it head-on.

I made a decision without even thinking. Instead of fighting the skid and trying to pull back into our lane, I spun the wheel to the left, aiming for the sidewalk on the other side of the truck.

For one sickening heartbeat, I thought we were dead. I braced, ready for the crash. And in the next second, we hit the edge of the sidewalk, hard enough for our seat belts to jerk us back on to the seats.

I kept my grip on the steering wheel, holding tight, trying to keep us on a straight line down the sidewalk.

Fire hydrant.

I spun the wheel again, cranking us back on to the street, missing the fire hydrant by less than the thickness of a coat of paint. We bounced off the sidewalk, shot through a gap of parked cars, and hit open pavement.

The van had opened its lead to a full block again.

I mashed the gas pedal and tried to catch up.

The van's brake lights showed red again. It made another turn to the right.

This time, I was ready for the corner. I eased off the gas, hitting the brakes hard. We rounded this corner under control.

I stomped the gas yet again, throwing us back against the bucket seats of the Jeep. In the next split second, I almost stood on the brakes.

We had rounded the corner to see a huge delivery truck angled across the street, backing into an alley. The delivery truck seemed to fill our entire windshield.

Five

I managed to stop a dozen steps from the side of the delivery truck. The blue van had not. It was resting sideways against the truck. The driver must have skidded sideways trying to stop and turn away from it. The van now blocked the delivery truck driver's door. The driver stared down at the top of the van from behind his own steering wheel.

"My brother!" Samantha shouted.

She yanked at the door handle and popped the door open. In her panic, she forgot the seat belt. It caught in her hair.

"Don't get out," I said.

"But my brother! He's in the van."

"The guys who kidnapped him are also in the—"

I snapped my mouth shut. The sliding door

on the van was opening, and they were getting out of the van. Two of them, not wearing ski masks now. The taller one had a walrus mustache. The shorter one had blond hair that reached his shoulders.

The one with the walrus mustache reached back with his free hand and dragged Ben from the van.

Without taking my eyes off them, I reached into the backseat. I knew exactly what I was going to grab. One of my hockey sticks on top of my gym bag.

I closed my hand on the shaft of wood and pulled the stick with me as I stepped out of the Jeep.

"Leave the kid," I said.

"Drop dead," the short, blond-haired guy said.

"Leave him." I wasn't going to let them take the kid.

"Drop dead," he repeated. "We'll give you the help you need to do it."

His partner pulled out a switchblade knife. He clicked it open.

Again, I felt a strange calmness. I gripped the stick like a baseball bat. I measured the distance between us. Instead of backing up, I took a step closer.

"Come on, boys," I said. "Try me out."

The second one pulled out a knife.

I grinned. A part of me wondered where my fearlessness was coming from. Another part of me got ready to swing hard and swing smart.

They split up. One moved to my left. One moved to my right. I couldn't defend myself against them both.

But the boy was free.

"Run hard, kid!" I shouted. "Take the chance now."

The boy sprinted toward me. Then passed me.

"You're meat," the guy with the mustache snarled, waving his knife. "Sliced, bloody meat."

"And you're a home run," I said, gripping my stick harder.

The sound of sirens reached us.

The men looked at each other and hesitated.

In that moment, I stepped forward and swung hard at the one on the right. He managed to get his arm up. I broke my stick across his forearm.

He shrieked.

Sirens rose louder.

The other one moved in close, stabbing at air.

I was left with half a hockey stick in my hands. I swung it at him, and he danced away.

His partner kept shrieking in agony.

I heard the Jeep's door slam shut.

"I'm with you!" Sam shouted.

"And me," a strange voice said. It belonged to the driver of the delivery truck, rounding the back of his vehicle. He carried a tire iron in his hand.

Both kidnappers reacted instantly. They ran across the street and into the alley.

I stared after them, suddenly aware that I was breathing hard and fast.

Time returned to normal speed. I began to realize what I had just done—I'd held my own against two men armed with switchblades.

"Leave them be," Sam said. "We got my brother back. We don't need to chase them."

I managed to nod. Like I was stupid enough to run after them?

"Sorry, kid," the truck driver growled. "It took me awhile to get out the passenger side of my truck. I had some boxes in the front seat."

He was a big man. Dirty blue jeans. Dirty black shirt. Big beer belly. I was glad he'd been on my side.

I managed to nod to him too. Had all of this really happened?

Sam's brother joined us. A kid with brown hair, his head hardly reached as high as her shoulders. He stood beside his sister, his arms wrapped around her waist. I found out later that Ben was allowed to participate in New Hope activities because his sister worked there.

"You don't speak much, do you?" Sam said to me.

"Um," I said. Something about her grin and the way her hair blew across her face tangled my heart and my tongue.

"What's your name anyway?" she asked.

"Um," I said again.

Where was my sense of calm when I really needed it?

Six

Hey, hero," Riley Judd told me, "prepare to look stupid."

We stood almost visor to visor at the center line during practice.

"Hero?" I asked. He stood on one side of the center line. I stood on the other.

"You didn't see me chasing down a van, did you? You didn't see me getting thank-you hugs from Sam."

I still couldn't believe I'd actually faced down two guys with switchblades the day before. I didn't expect anyone on the team to believe it either. They'd probably give me stupid nickname and I'd never hear the end of it. I preferred to be invisible. A person stayed out of trouble that way.

"How many times do I have to tell you it

wasn't a big deal," I said. "Sam was probably just happy to get her brother back and—"

The piercing blast of Coach Fink's whistle interrupted me.

"You clowns going to gab all afternoon?" Coach asked as he skated toward us. "Or are you ready to play?"

"Ready to play," I said. "Sorry, Coach."

"Play?" Riley Judd said. He pushed his helmet back to look me directly in the face. "Play? I'm ready to put on a show."

I sure hoped he wouldn't. For the first half hour, we had skated hard during this practice. We had then spent twenty minutes in shooting drills, another twenty minutes in passing drills. Now we would finish with a half hour of scrimmage. Blue against teal—half the team against the other half in a game situation.

During the entire scrimmage, our fourth line would play against the first line. When we rested, the second and third lines would play each other. We would continue to alternate until the end of the scrimmage.

I wore a blue jersey. Riley Judd wore the teal. If Riley did put on a show, it would be directly against the blues. Worse, Riley was my man to guard. If he played great, the person looking like a fool would be me.

It didn't take him long to embarrass me.

The puck went into their end. Riley took a pass from the defenseman, and skated directly toward me with the puck.

I must have been frowning with concentration, because he glanced at my face and laughed.

"Not a chance," he said. "Watch this."

He faked a pass to his center, Blake Sundeen. I didn't go for the fake. It would have been better if I had.

Instead of trying to slide the puck past me, Riley snapped a quick hard wrist shot into the middle of my belly.

"Oof," I said, clutching myself as the puck dropped between my skates.

Riley snaked his stick ahead of him, pushed the puck all the way through my skates, cut around me, and cruised down the boards*. His laughter echoed throughout the empty arena.

His wasn't the only laughter, though. The rest of the guys found it funny too.

I wish that had been the only time he made me look dumb.

But no, it seemed every time he touched the puck, he showed me another unbelievable move to sucker me.

In a way, though, I had to admire him. At ice level, playing against him, I was able to understand what made him a superstar, although just by looking at him, you wouldn't think he was one of the greats. He wasn't as big as most of the players. He wasn't as fast. He didn't have an overpowering shot.

Instead, he seemed to have a sixth sense that told him where everybody was on the ice. It was like all ten skaters were players on a chess board, and he knew every move each of them would make and where the puck would go.

To go along with his uncanny ability to read each developing play, he could handle the puck as if it were nailed to the end of his hockey stick. He didn't need to be big or fast or overpowering. He slipped and slid through crowds of players as if he were oil poured through marbles, and when he reached open ice on the other side of the crowd, the puck would still be on his stick.

It was actually fun to watch him. Although it would have been nice to have him on my line instead of against me.

No matter what I did, he got past me. In fact, he scored ten goals during the scrimmage.

I don't usually get frustrated. Trouble was, every time he beat me, he laughed.

With two minutes left in the scrimmage, it was the same old situation. Puck behind their net.

Defenseman Ryan Hampson passed the puck to Riley. I had to go chase him.

This time, Riley went to my right. He stopped, spun around backward, flipped the puck between his legs in the opposite direction, jumped over my stick and found open ice again.

I screamed in frustration.

Again, laughter.

I put my head down and chased him hard.

At their blue line, I almost caught him. Until he put on a little burst of speed and slipped away. At the center line, I almost caught him again. He danced just out of reach. At our blue line, he slowed and I nearly reached him.

He laughed again. I realized he was slowing down just to give me a chance.

I screamed again. No way was he going to score goal number eleven.

But he did. He cut to the inside and lifted his stick to let the puck stop. He kicked it ahead with a skate back onto his stick. Then he fired a low hard screamer into the left side of the net, using the defenseman to screen the goalie.

I screamed yet again.

The goalie dug the puck out of the net and flipped it toward me.

I was so mad that as the puck reached me, I half turned, dropped my head and blasted a slap shot* away from all the players into the corner boards.

Only just as the puck was leaving my stick and just as I was lifting my head to see where the puck was going, I noticed trouble. Big trouble.

Our Assistant Coach Talafous, thinking he was well out of the way of the scrimmage, had drifted into the corner. His hands were in his pockets. Right where my hundred-mile-an-hour slap shot was about to hit.

For that split second, we stared at each other. I wondered if my face had the same expression of horror that his face did. Because we both knew the puck was headed for an area a few inches below his belt buckle.

Coach Talafous made a big mistake. He should have tried to block the puck by pulling his hands out of his pockets. Instead, he jumped up, hoping the puck would go between his legs.

It didn't.

The puck drilled him solid. Right where his legs joined together.

His face showed instant disbelief. The kind of disbelief that comes when you know that you've been hit there, but you don't feel the pain yet because it is still traveling up your body. But you know how bad it's going to be and any second the pain's going to reach your brain.

It reached his brain. His face puckered as he tried to get air. He doubled over, sagging to the ice like a deflating beach ball.

Coach Talafous curled up on the ice and moaned in agony.

Riley skated up to me and tapped me on the shoulder.

"Nice shot, Watson," he said. "But shooting drills ended a half hour ago."

It took Coach Talafous fifteen minutes to get to his feet again. The first thing Coach Fink did was to tell me to get my skates off and start running with all the rest of my equipment on. I heard him ask the strength coach to come up with something creative for me to do the rest of the practice. Then he said we'd be sure to talk about maintaining discipline and which stats I'd be keeping from the stands during the league game on Sunday. So much for trying to stay invisible and out of trouble.

Seven

On Tuesday, Riley and I made another visit to New Hope Mission.

During the game I watched from the stands, Riley had managed to collect three goals, two assists, business cards from every scout in attendance, and what seemed like a file a couple of inches thick of newspaper clippings.

Me? I had managed to collect a cold from a lady who sneezed on me in the first game, and popcorn in my hair from a kid who had spilled his bucket during the second game.

I thought about this as I parked the Jeep near the old brick church building. I was not in a good mood to be baby-sitting Riley Judd through another visit to New Hope.

I was in a worse mood after an hour and a half with the little monsters of our assigned group.

"Are they always like this?" I asked Samantha. She had just walked into the room to check on our group. Youth Works was big enough that she supervised volunteers working with kids in five different age groups. Today, Riley and I were stuck with just the eight- and nine-year-olds.

Although my stomach still danced with nervousness around her, I was finally able to speak to her without my teeth getting in the way of my tongue. It must have helped that I remembered how she had spent ten minutes hugging me for helping to save her brother from the guys with knives.

Samantha surveyed the room with me. It was the size of a regular classroom, tucked in a back hall of the church building. It had old couches, posters of rock stars on the wall, and fifteen kids jumping, screaming, and spitting paper wads at each other.

"You can speak!" she said with mock surprise.

"Last week I had, um, a dentist appointment," I said. I decided the floor would be interesting to stare at. Maybe I really could speak to her, but I couldn't quite look her right in those beautiful eyes. "My mouth was frozen when we got here. That's why I didn't say much. Really."

She grinned, like she knew that I knew that she knew that I was making it up.

"Anyway," she said, "these kids are on good behavior today. They think it's cool you guys are hockey players."

"Well," I said, "at least one of us is."

"What?" she asked.

"Nothing." Hockey was a depressing subject to me. So I changed it. "Your brother okay after last week?"

She nodded. A pillow flew over our heads.

"Any idea why those guys took him?" I hadn't had a chance to talk to her. After the police had shown up—interrupting the hug that I was enjoying so much—we had become too busy answering their questions to speak to each other.

"No idea," she said. She raised her voice to a couple of grimy-faced kids. "Bobby, take your hands off Sahid's neck!"

Bobby grinned. Sahid grinned. Bobby let go of Sahid's neck. Sahid promptly grabbed Bobby's neck.

"These kids are something," she said. "This group is full of kids who have real trouble in school."

She shook her head in sympathy for them. "But they really have had a tough life for such short lives. That kid's parents hit him or yell at

43

him all the time. Some don't get a decent meal for days. Others are even left alone for days, while their parents wander the bars. And a lot of them have serious medical problems. Yet somehow they have turned out to be like most any other group of kids. How can we expect to make a difference with so few workers?"

"Yeah," I said, not sure if I meant it. To me, they looked like brats. Three of them had jumped on Riley, and he was staggering around with them hanging from his waist and shoulders.

"No idea why those guys kidnapped your brother?" I repeated. "How about the van? Did you find out who it belonged to?"

"Micah!" she yelled. "I know it's a nerf bat, but it can still hurt."

The kid grinned and kept whacking another boy over the head with the soft foam bat.

"The police told me it belonged to some pharmaceutical company," she answered as if we hadn't been interrupted.

"Pharmaceutical companies are into kidnapping?"

She laughed. "No, silly. The van had been stolen from the company."

"Oh."

Her face suddenly showed alarm, and she looked around the room wildly. "Ben! Where's

Ben!"

Her little brother was not among the kids jumping around this room.

I put my fingers in my mouth and whistled. Loud.

It froze most of the kids as if I had shot a gun. The three kids on Riley dropped to the ground. Micah gave his little buddy one final whack with the nerf bat.

"Listen up," I said. "Where's Ben?"

"Here."

Samantha and I looked around, but we couldn't spot where the voice had come from.

"Where?"

"Here!" He crawled out from behind the couch. Dust balls clung to his hair and his clothes. "I was looking for a marble."

Samantha grabbed my hand with her cool fingers. She let out a deep breath. I hadn't realized how scared she was until then. She let go of my hand, probably not even knowing she'd grabbed it. I knew, though.

The little monsters began to bounce around the room again, screaming and yelling. I began to feel like the "before" part of a headache commercial.

"This is nuts," I muttered. I doubt anyone heard me. Not even Samantha, who was still close beside me.

I put my fingers to my mouth and whistled

again.

It froze them all again. Except for Micah, who continued to hammer his friend with the nerf bat. I walked over and yanked it from him. He glared at me, but didn't say a thing.

"Listen up," I barked. I waved the bat in a general circle. "You are going to learn to do something with your energy. And it won't have anything to do with this chaos."

"Oh yeah?" some kid asked.

At the back of the room, another volunteer wheeled in a cart with a giant Kool-Aid container and plates of cookies. I knew I wouldn't have the attention of these kids much longer.

"Yeah," I said. "You guys know Riley Judd is the best hockey player in the MJHL?"

"Maybe," the same kid said.

"You'd better believe it," I said, pointing the end of the baseball bat at the kid and looking him right in the eyes. "So you should consider yourselves pretty lucky."

"Um, why?" the kid asked in a quieter voice.

"Because he's going to teach you to play roller hockey."

The kids erupted in big cheers.

Samantha, standing beside me, leaned over to make sure no one overheard her. "Don't make promises you can't keep, Tyler Watson.

You don't know how good you have it compared to some of these kids. I don't want to see you hurting them."

Riley pushed his way through them and put his face right up to mine.

"No way in the world I'm going to teach them anything," he said. "You've lost your mind."

"Got any better ideas for passing time around here?"

He frowned.

The kids continued cheering. This was a big deal to them.

"Besides," I said. "Do you really have the heart to tell them you won't?"

"I'll get you for this," he said.

"You already did," I told him. "Remember?

Eight

I've still got one game left in my suspension."

"He shoots! He scores!" Riley yelled, a big grin on his face.

Except this was one of the few times Riley himself wasn't scoring. Instead, it was Micah, the little kid who loved to whack his friends with a nerf bat. Micah had just hit a wobbly slap shot three inches high. The only reason he had scored was because the goalie—an eight-year-old—had thick glasses and could hardly see.

The audience to this street hockey game consisted of two people—Riley and me. We were both in sneakers and Northern Lights sweats, standing at the side of a paved courtyard in the shadow of the mission building, watching the kids bump a ball around with cut-down hockey sticks.

Micah ran up to us and grinned back at Riley, then licked his upper lip because his nose was runny.

"Great goal," Riley said. "I sincerely mean it."

"Don't lick that stuff," I told Micah. "Wipe it with your sleeve. Real hockey players always wipe with their sleeves."

"No they don't," Riley said. "They do this."

Riley pinched one nostril shut by pressing a finger against it. Then he pointed his face away from us and blew an explosive snort to spray his other nostril clear. "See?"

"Cool," Micah said. He grinned again and nodded, then ran back to join the others in the street hockey game.

"Good example, Riley," I said. We had a gym bag filled with water bottles and towels near our feet. I reached down, grabbed a bottle, and squirted some water into my mouth.

He leaned on his hockey stick. "Someone's got to teach these poor kids some manners."

"If I didn't know better," I said, "I'd think you almost cared."

"Don't tell anyone," he replied, "but I do. These kids can grow on you."

I nodded in agreement as the two of us kept our eyes on the kids.

It was now early November. In the last two weeks, Riley Judd had firmly established himself as the league's top scorer. No surprise, I had firmly established myself as the team's fourth-line right winger. For the third year in a row.

And in these two weeks, Riley and I had firmly established ourselves as heroes among these kids—even though I'd made a mistake by promising them roller hockey without first realizing how much it would cost to get them all into in-line skates. So we had told them it would be safer to first learn the basics of stickhandling by playing street hockey in sneakers.

Fortunately they were just as happy with a bunch of old hockey sticks and the rules of street hockey, which we made simple for them. Rule one—hit the ball, not someone else. Rule two—try to knock the ball between the big rocks we set up as goal posts at each end of the courtyard. Rule three—no other rules.

What I found sad was how little it had taken to become heroes to these kids. Some of them had such terrible family lives away from New Hope that these street hockey games became the highlight of their week.

"What do you say, Tyler?" Riley asked, interrupting my thoughts. "Should we show these kids how the real hockey guys play?"

"Yup." I dropped the water bottle back into the gym bag.

Among cheers from the kids, Riley jogged to one end of the courtyard, and I jogged to the other end. I realized something else had happened in the last two weeks. Riley and I had drifted into a friendship. He was still a showboat, and I was still invisible, but when it was just the two of us—like here or driving in my Jeep—the differences didn't seem as great. If you ignored Riley's cockiness, he was almost likable.

"Okay, boys," Riley shouted as he got the ball, "pour it on!"

A gang of kids moved on him like ants on honey. We not only had the eight- and nine-year-olds, but also a good group of twelve- and thirteen-year-olds today. Our task wouldn't be easy.

Riley's arms and legs flashed as he danced around, slapping the ball back and forth with his stick. Somehow —and I doubt a slow motion replay could have showed how—Riley made it through the maze of players with the ball. He shouted and screamed as their sticks hit his shins, but he made it through. He kept the ball for five minutes, running in circles as the kids on both teams chased him and yipped in glee.

Finally, Riley stopped running in circles and headed toward where I guarded the goal at the open end of the courtyard.

I got ready to stop him.

Riley stopped, grinned, and flipped me the ball.

"I'm tired. Your turn."

"Thanks," I said.

The horde of kids moved on me.

I don't have the stickhandling skills that Riley does.

I decided instead to rely on keeping my distance from them.

Instead of heading toward Riley's net, I backed up, keeping the ball with me.

The paved courtyard was U-shaped. At Riley's end was the church office. On both sides, three-story walls. On my side, the opening led into an empty parking lot.

They were coming at me like a pack of insane wolves.

I turned and bolted toward the empty parking lot, keeping the ball in front of me.

"Hey!" a couple of kids shouted.

"Get him!" a couple more shouted.

They all screamed and began to chase me.

This was fun.

I outran them easily, building my lead to at least twenty-five steps. When I reached the far end of the parking lot, I turned and faced them.

They were a wave of street warriors, yelling

and grinning and waving their sticks, ready to pounce.

I waited until they were almost on me. Then I flipped the ball over their heads and ran around them, chasing down the ball toward my own net and the courtyard.

"Breeaaakkkaaawaayyyyy!" I yelled. And it was a breakaway. Longer than any breakaway in the history of hockey. The kids had turned to stampede after me, but they were well behind me. I had the empty parking lot ahead, all of the courtyard, and finally, far, far away, there was Riley at the other net, leaning on his stick and waiting for me to arrive.

I thundered toward him. I didn't need any fancy stickwork at this point. We used a street hockey ball—made of orange plastic and heavier than a hockey puck. It wasn't going to get stuck in the cracks of the pavement.

When I reached my own net again—with all of the courtyard ahead of me and the kids now thirty steps behind—I yelled, "Riley, prepare for the shot of doom!"

"Tyler," he yelled back, "you don't have a chance!"

I kept sprinting toward him. Then, without warning, I stopped. Close enough to have a good chance at scoring. Far enough away so that Riley would still have time to make the save if he was fast enough.

I set the ball up carefully and backed up two steps.

Riley knew exactly what I was going to do. He set himself up like a goaltender.

The kids were yelling and screaming.

"Ready, Riley?"

"Sure, marshmallow man!" he said, insulting my slap shot even before I hit it.

"Marshmallow?" I roared back.

The kids were almost on me. I couldn't wait any longer.

I raised my stick above my head, took the two steps, and timed it perfectly so that I was bringing the stick down and launching my body weight into the world's biggest, baddest slap shot.

Nine

I crunched that ball with everything I had.

And I watched it soar over Riley's head to smash directly through a window behind him.

"Oops," I said. I waited for someone to yell through the window at me.

Nothing.

The kids gathered around me.

"Well," I said, reminding myself I was supposed to be a good example, "I'd better go tell someone what I did."

"Hey, Tyler," little Micah said at the back of the crowd.

"Yeah?"

"When you're in there, if it looks like you're going to be in big trouble, can you at least throw us the ball?"

"Huh?"

"This street hockey is fun," he explained.

"We want to keep playing."

"Thanks for the support," I said.

He nodded. I guess kids at that age have a tough time understanding sarcasm.

I waved at Riley. "See you in a few minutes."

"Tell you what," he said, "let them know we'll both pay for the window."

"It was my shot," I said.

He shrugged. "Our game."

I grinned. Riley was getting more human all the time.

I waved again and trotted toward the side doors that would let me inside the church building.

◆

It wasn't difficult to find the office with the broken window. All I did was walk down the hallway and open doors until I found a room with natural air conditioning.

Finding the ball, however, wasn't so easy. There was no one inside the office to tell me where it went.

I saw gray steel filing cabinets against one wall. I saw a big gray steel desk in the corner of the other two walls. I saw a crooked chair on swivel wheels. I saw broken glass sprayed on the yellow tile floor. But I didn't see an orange hockey ball.

I dropped to my knees.

Naturally, the ball had rolled beneath the desk, right into the far corner.

I looked around for something to use to reach the ball.

Nothing.

I'd have to get on my hands and knees and crawl.

I pushed the chair away and crawled into the opening beneath the center of the desk. I bent lower and reached into the corner. My fingertips just barely touched the ball. I stretched farther.

Then I heard footsteps in the hallway, coming in my direction. And I heard voices. I recognized one voice as Samantha's.

How good would this look, me with my hind end pointing at the ceiling?

I grunted and stretched as far as I could, finally able to get enough of the ball to roll it toward me. I grabbed the ball and backed out.

My sleeve snagged on a screw that poked out of the bottom of the desk.

The voices grew louder.

For a moment, I nearly yanked hard. But it felt like I was stuck good, and I didn't want to rip my Northern Lights jacket.

The voices moved past the open door and continued down the hallway. Two voices. Two sets of footsteps. The other voice belonged to a man. I didn't recognize his voice.

There was a click as the door to the office next to me opened.

"Step inside, Samantha," I heard the man's voice say. The clearness of the sound surprised me. Then I saw the vent on the wall, just inches from my face. I easily guessed that's how I was able to hear.

I was still stuck, though. I tried wiggling my arm. It didn't help.

"I don't understand what this is about," Samantha told him.

I didn't want to listen. Their conversation was none of my business. I made myself into a pretzel and tried to reach my sleeve with my other arm.

"Sit down," the voice said. "It's about your brother."

I heard her gasp. "He's all right, isn't he?"

"Yes," the man's voice said, "for now."

I frowned. His voice did not sound pleasant.

"You're still asking around about the kids," the voice said. "Didn't you get the note telling you to stop?"

"But—"

"But nothing. It wasn't an accident that your brother was taken. It was a warning. Even if the muscle-brained jerk with the hockey stick

58

hadn't gotten in the way, your brother would have been returned the next day."

"Tyler? He's not a—"

"Listen to me, Samantha. Listen good. You stop asking questions. Otherwise next time something permanent will happen to your brother. You could go to the newspapers. You could go to the police. You could let the whole world know about this. But the injury to your brother would already be done. Understand?"

I'd stopped caring about my sleeve.

There was long silence in the other office.

Finally Samantha answered the man. "I understand," she said.

"That's a smart girl."

There was a scraping of chairs.

He must have stood. Which meant they were leaving. Which also meant they might see me as they left the office.

I pushed hard, trying to get the rest of me under the desk.

Neither of them spoke as they left the office next door. One set of footsteps headed one way. Another set headed the other. No footsteps stopped at this office and looked in to find me under the desk.

To get free, I had to slide and bend and work myself loose from my jacket. I backed out, then crawled in from another angle to unhook the sleeve from the screw. Then I tossed the ball down to the courtyard.

The waiting kids cheered.

Cheering or not, I didn't feel better.

On my way outside, I passed the office where Samantha and the man had been talking.

It didn't help my mood.

The sign on the door showed that the office belonged to Earl Chadley, director of New Hope.

Ten

An hour later, when we got into the Jeep, Riley reached into the gym bag. He tossed the water bottle into my lap.

"Kool-Aid," he said.

I started the Jeep and began to drive.

I didn't start drinking.

"Aren't you thirsty? We ran those kids ragged. I hope we'll have energy for practice."

"Yeah," I said. It was six o'clock. We had a half hour to get to the rink and another half hour to get dressed in hockey equipment for one of the few night practices of the year. We would have a light practice because tomorrow was a game day.

Riley guzzled from his own water bottle. He smacked his lips. "Good stuff," he said. "I borrowed it from their snack cart. You know, the one with the cookies and big Kool-Aid jugs that shows up for the kids."

"Yeah," I said.

"I guess you can't really say we're borrowing this Kool-Aid," Riley said. "I mean, they probably wouldn't want it back when we're through with it. Or when it gets through us."

"Yeah," I said, finally drinking some Kool-Aid from my own water bottle.

"What's the matter?" Riley asked. "I just made a joke."

I drank in silence.

"Did Samantha turn you down?" he continued. There was a student social coming up at Normandale Community College. I'd made the mistake yesterday of mentioning to Riley that I'd like to take Sam to it.

"Didn't ask her," I said. At least I hadn't asked her about going with me. After tracking her down, I'd told her about the window. Then I had worked up enough courage to ask her why her brother was in danger. She'd gotten angry and told me to mind my own business.

"You've got to go for it," Riley said. "Only two weeks."

I turned a corner and headed onto 35W South.

"She might say no," I said. My mind,

though, was on Earl Chadley, director of New Hope. Riley and I had met him only briefly. He had introduced himself to us on our second visit and thanked us for our help with a big smile that didn't seem real.

Earl Chadley was a skinny man with long hair that he flipped back while he was speaking. He wore sandals and blue jeans and a ratty old shirt, which might have been cool if he were twenty instead of closer to fifty.

Why was he threatening Samantha Blair with something as serious as hurting her brother? What secret did she know that she was supposed to keep hidden? What were the questions she wasn't supposed to ask?

"Hey, Watson, snap out of it," Riley said, "I was telling you something."

"Sure," I said. "What?"

"It's advice," Riley said. "The only way you get anywhere in life is by taking chances."

"Sure," I said.

He snapped his fingers. "It's the window, right? You're bummed out about that. I already told you, I'll pay for half the damage."

"Don't worry about it," I said. My mind was still on Samantha and the weird conversation I had overheard. "There are a lot worse things in life than broken windows."

I found myself yawning as we skated our warm-up patterns to begin the practice.

I moved past a bunch of guys leaning and stretching from side to side to loosen up. I put on a burst of speed past Almquist, Hanus, and Marshall catching up to Riley.

"I think it was a dumb idea to play street hockey before practice," I said, cruising beside him. "My legs feel like wooden stilts."

Riley didn't answer.

"Hey! Goofball. Didn't you hear me?"

He turned his face toward me. He had a strange frown. It crunched his face into a look of worry.

"You all right?" I asked.

He stumbled, then caught his balance. "I don't know."

He stumbled again.

Now panic crossed his face.

"Tyler!" I heard fear in his voice.

Someone fired a pass in our direction. The puck bounced off his skates.

"Tyler!"

"I'm right beside you," I said. The fear in his voice scared me too.

"Skate closer," he said. "Let me grab your arm."

I moved tight beside him. With his hockey glove still on, he pulled at my sweater.

"Get me to the players' bench," he said. "Move slowly, so it looks like we're talking about stuff."

"I don't get it," I said.

"Just do it, all right?"

Guys skated past us. Singer and Deutsch were already moving at full speed, getting ready for the regular skating drills that Coach Fink used to keep us in shape.

I felt like a boy scout helping an old lady across the street.

"We there yet?" he asked.

"Don't be dumb," I said. "You can look for yourself."

"No," he said. "I can't."

"Huh?"

"Tyler," he said. "I have weird allergies. Sometimes they act up. But never this bad."

He stumbled a bit.

"I'm scared," he said, "real scared. I can't see. It's like the whole world is gray."

Eleven

It took Riley an hour to get his vision back. Although he could see again, he was no longer the same person he'd been before. I discovered that a few days later as we were driving toward New Hope for our next visit. Riley turned down the volume of the car stereo.

"Why you listen to country music is beyond me," he said.

I took my right hand off the steering wheel and turned the volume up again. "Because I can understand the words."

I braked hard to miss a truck that had suddenly slowed in the left lane.

He took advantage of the distraction and turned the volume down again. "Words? That's dumb. It's called listening to music, remember? You jam a CD in your stereo and listen to music. Not words."

Safely past the truck, I turned onto Lake Street, toward New Hope. I also turned up the volume. Again. "It's not music when the singers are screeching like they've slammed their fingers in a door."

He turned the knob down. Again. "Sometimes you act like an old man," he said. "'Screeching singers' is something my dad would say."

I turned it up. "I act like an old man?"

He turned it down. "Yeah, an old man. Like you don't want to take chances."

I turned it up. "If I need a psychologist, you'll be the first person I call."

He turned the volume down.

"Riley . . ." It wasn't funny anymore.

"Could be I'm the one who needs a psychologist," he said. His voice was quiet and serious. "Do you think about God? About dying?"

I left the volume turned down. Maybe I hadn't heard him right. "Dying?"

"Dying," he repeated.

I let the word hang in the air, trying to decide what to say. I believed in God. But I didn't know what to say to Riley. So I just listened.

"Look," he said, "I trust you. But if you ever tell any of the guys on the team I started talking about this, I'll kill you."

"I won't say anything. But why are you thinking about—"

"Dying?"

"Yeah," I said. "I mean, we're hockey players. We're not supposed to think that hard."

"We're also not supposed to suddenly go blind for an hour for no reason at all."

"I agree," I said. "That was weird."

It had been weird. Although a couple of days had passed, the doctors were still no closer to figuring out what had happened to Riley during practice.

"Tyler, I'll admit I was scared when everything went gray. You know that."

For the next few seconds we both thought about his losing his sight as I slowed the Jeep in front of the New Hope building. I pulled on the parking brake and half opened my door.

Riley's voice stopped me.

"Nothing like that ever happened to me before," Riley said. "I've never felt helpless like that. I was blind for an hour, but I didn't know if my vision would ever come back. Now, I keep wondering if I'll suddenly go blind again. And what if I stay blind?"

"Well, you could always get a job as a referee."

"This is not the time to be funny," he said.

I snapped my mouth shut.

"So I started thinking about my heart," Riley continued. "I mean, there it is, pumping blood all by itself without me telling it to. What if it stopped all of a sudden, for no reason—just like I went blind for no reason. For that matter, why does my heart keep beating? Every night since then, I haven't been able to fall asleep because when I think about my heart stopping, I think about dying and what happens after that."

The Jeep door was still half open. I closed it. "Don't get me wrong," I said. "But is that why you've played the last two games so badly?"

Riley had managed only one assist in two games. Both games had been against the visiting Northwest Wisconsin Knights. We'd won 8–5 and 10–6, and Riley had only scored one point out of the combined 18 goals. Even the newspaper articles had begun to question his slump.

"My confidence is gone," he said. "Can you blame me? If my eyes can go, anything else can go. I half expect to go blind during a shift. Or keel over from a heart attack as I rush up the ice."

"It was a freak thing," I said. "Like getting hit by lightning."

He snorted. "Let me ask you this. If you got hit by lighting once and survived, wouldn't you be nervous to be outside in a thunderstorm again?"

I was beginning to understand his fear.

"You didn't get any warning about losing your sight, did you?"

"No," he said. "And I'd give almost anything to know why it happened."

◆

"Listen up, guys," I shouted to get the kids' attention. "Weather looks good out there today. Anyone want to play some street hockey?"

As expected, they cheered. I didn't blame them. The New Hope lot was small and crowded. Normal kids would go crazy in here. And as Riley and I had learned during our visits here, this bunch was definitely so hyperactive they were beyond normal.

"Riley's got the sticks," I shouted. "Let's not tear down the hallways as we go outside. Zip your lips and line up in single file."

I couldn't believe what happened next.

The kids stopped shouting and laughing and screaming and began to line up in single file.

Riley gave me a surprised look.

"They must like hockey," I said.

I stayed at the door, and Riley led them out.

I watched Ben, Samantha's brother. He was in the middle of the line. When he passed me, I patted his shoulder.

"How you doing?" I said. What I really wanted to ask him was if anyone had tried to kidnap him for the second time. I really wanted to ask him if he knew why the director of Youth Works was threatening his sister.

"I'm doing good," he said. "Can I be a goalie today?"

"Sure," I said. "Hey, what's with the cotton ball?"

He was wearing a T-shirt, and the cotton ball was obvious, taped to the inside bend of his elbow. I'd had the same thing myself after donating blood to the Red Cross.

"Blood tests," he said, like it was no big deal. "We all get them. Samantha says I have to leave it on until after dinner."

"Oh."

He marched onward. I followed him out of

the room and down the hallway. I kept my eyes open for Samantha. She was always running around and doing different things around the building. If I was lucky, I could run into her and find an excuse to ask her to the Normandale student night. There was only a week left. I didn't have the courage to call her by telephone.

But I didn't see her.

Fifteen minutes later, I had bigger things to worry about.

Micah, my favorite little red-head monster kid, stopped in his tracks in the middle of the courtyard. He toppled to his side as one of the other kids fired him a pass.

His head made a horrible sound as it hit the pavement. His body began to flop around. I got there just as his face was turning blue. Riley arrived a half second later.

"Ambulance?" Riley asked.

"Yes, hurry!" I said. This was no time to ask any other questions or think about anything else.

Riley dashed toward the New Hope offices.

I dropped to my knees and leaned over Joey. He was wheezing, like he couldn't breathe.

I whipped off my jacket and folded it as a pillow beneath his neck. I pinched his nostrils together with the thumb and forefinger of my right hand. I pulled his chin down with my other hand. His face was cold and clammy.

"You'll be all right, little buddy," I said with a lot more calm than I felt. "Let's just get you breathing right again."

I began to blow air into his lungs.

Twelve

Sunday afternoon, as the referee skated into the faceoff* circle deep in our end, I looked at the score board. Seven to six. We were leading this home game against the Dubuque Thunderbirds. Ten minutes, twenty-seven seconds left in the game. A full house of screaming fans.

The players had lined up, waiting for the puck to drop. I didn't feel my usual nervousness. In the second period, I had scored a goal. I had tipped in a slap shot from one of our defensemen at the point. By scoring that goal, I knew Coach Fink would see that I could contribute to this game.

I turned my attention away from the score clock and back to the game.

The referee slapped the puck down between

the sticks of the centers. They fought for the puck. Our center spun his body around, blocking the other center. Our center kicked the puck back with his skate, sending it to our defenseman who was waiting behind the net.

By then, I was already moving toward the boards. As winger, that was my position. If we lost the puck and it squirted up to their defenseman on the blue line, I was close enough to keep him from shooting at our goalie. If we kept the puck, I was in position to take a pass.

This time, our defenseman Tim Hansen fired the puck along the boards.

It began to bounce, and I knew I would have trouble trapping it with my stick. I backed up against the boards and turned my skates to trap the puck.

Unfortunately, this gave their defenseman time to rush down the boards toward me. He reached me just as the puck did. He hit me with a full body check, and spun me around.

I should have thanked him. He slid off me and fell to his knees. I ended up facing their net. And the puck was straight ahead, waiting like a plum for me to pick off a branch.

I sprinted forward. The crowd's roar grew. They could see what I saw.

Two of us Northern Lights forwards. Only one defenseman left to protect the net at the far end. We had a two-on-one* breakaway!

I flipped the pass over to Andy Mulholland, the other winger, who had cruised into the open ice at center. He busted ahead at an angle, drawing the defenseman over to the side. I was skating at full speed too.

Mulholland and I had at least a ten-step head start on the next closest Thunderbird.

Wind filled my face; the roar of the crowd shook my whole body.

I kept to the middle of the ice, and when Andy and I crossed their blue line, I began to slow down. Just a bit. That forced the defenseman into making a move. He had to go wide to stay with Andy, or slow down to stay with me. If he stayed with me, Andy could go in alone on the goalie. If he moved to Andy, I would be free for a wide-open pass.

The defenseman decided to gamble. He stayed with Andy as long as he could, and as Andy went to backhand me a pass, the defenseman dove, hoping to block it.

The puck slid beneath him. Onto my stick.

I was at the top of their faceoff circle. Just me and the goalie. And hundreds of fans screaming for me to bury the puck in the net.

It was the big chance to be a hero, and I didn't want it.

What if I tripped? What if I missed the net? I'd be a bum.

I faked my head and shoulders to the left, dragged the puck to the right, and went to fire a cannon of a wristshot. Except the puck hopped over my stick and rolled back into my skates.

Desperate to take a shot, I kicked it ahead. I took a feeble slap at the puck and managed to hit a slow looping shot that the goalie gloved easily.

Not only had I missed scoring, but I had also missed in the ugliest way possible. And in front of nearly every person in Minnesota who cared about junior hockey.

The ref blew the whistle to stop the play. I hung my head in the sudden silence of the disappointed crowd and got off the ice as soon as I could.

Thirteen

Coach Fink didn't say a word as I reached the players' bench. He didn't have to. I had a good idea of what was going through his mind.

After the game, Coach Fink took me aside in the hallway and spoke with me briefly. What he told me did not put me in a great mood. He wanted to meet with me on Wednesday morning after dryland. I doubted he wanted to move me up to the first or second line, even if Riley was still playing badly.

Unfortunately, when I left the coach I had to hide my sour mood because Micah and his mother were waiting for me in the lobby of the ice arena. I had told Micah I'd meet them after the game for burgers and milkshakes.

It had taken the team awhile to shower and to listen to the coach's post-game talk, so the lobby was nearly deserted. Micah and his mother saw me right away and walked in my direction. Micah looked fine, which was amazing considering that earlier in the week he had spent a night in the hospital hooked up to a breathing machine.

"Hey, Tyler," Micah said. He gave me a high five, which I returned. I had visited him at the hospital, and when I found out they were releasing him, I had given him a pair of tickets to today's game.

His mother stood beside him. She was short, wearing an old jacket. Her hair was blond and stringy, her face pale and splotchy. I smelled cigarette smoke on her clothes.

"I'm Judith Scranton," she said. She bit her lower lip, "Micah's mother, but you probably guessed that."

"Hello," I told her. "I'm glad you were able to bring Micah to the game."

She shrugged. "You got us the tickets."

Her attitude threw me. Chances were good, the doctor had said, that I had saved her kid's life by giving him mouth-to-mouth. I'd given him hockey tickets. But it was like she didn't care. She looked every direction but in my eyes. She didn't smile. She fidgeted.

"Let's go," Micah said. "Tyler said we could get burgers and shakes."

"I told you," she hissed at him. "We can't afford it."

"My treat," I told them.

"No," she said. "You already done plenty. I'm not going to owe you more."

"But—"

"Nope. We may be poor, but we don't need charity from strangers."

"Mom . . ." Micah said. He was squirming.

"But Mrs. Scranton—"

"Ms., if you don't mind. And if Micah and I don't hurry, we'll miss our bus."

Bus? This wasn't an easy place to reach by bus, not from the part of Minneapolis where they lived. By giving them the tickets, I'd forced her to spend hours on a bus?

"I can give you a ride," I said.

She shook her head no. "We'll be fine."

"But—"

"We'll be fine," she said. It began to dawn on me that she was very uncomfortable around me. It also began to dawn on me that I felt uncomfortable around her.

Here I was, in nice new dress pants, polished dress shoes, a leather jacket, and with a haircut that might have cost more than the old coat she wore. Micah's dirty clothes were little more than rags, his fingernails and hair were grubby, and there were holes in his

80

running shoes.

Was her life so tough that she didn't want to be reminded of another world, where teenaged kids had Jeeps to drive and she was forced to take the bus?

"It was nice meeting you," I finally said.

"You too," she said, her lips tight. I wondered how much begging Micah had done just to get her to the game.

"See you later, Micah," I said. "Down at New Hope, right? Get ready for some big-time street hockey."

"No," Mrs. Scranton said. "You won't see him there."

"I beg your pardon?"

"You won't see him there." Her voice became angry. "First they pay me to get Micah in the program. And right when it seems things are finally right with him, they kick him out."

I looked at Micah. He nodded, with a miserable look on his face.

"Yeah," he said. "First Nathan and Rashawn and Jamie. Now me. It ain't fair."

"I don't get it," I said. "Nathan and Rashawn and Jamie. Who are they?"

"Kids," he said. "New Hope kids. They got sent to the hospital too. Just like me."

"Just like you?"

He nodded gravely. "Yup. Seizures."

Mrs. Scranton glared at me like it was my fault Joey was out of New Hope. She pulled Joey away and headed for the exit, leaving me to stare at them with an open mouth.

Four kids with seizures?

They were almost to the outer doors by the time I caught up to them.

"Mrs. Scranton," I said, "would you mind if Micah told me the last names of those other three kids?"

Fourteen

I marched into Sam's office. It was exactly a week since Micah had had his seizure.

"I'd like you to tell me what is going on," I said to her.

Without getting up from her desk, she looked at her watch. "Well, for the next two hours, you and Riley will be playing street hockey with the boys." She smiled. "I can't tell you how much it has meant to them. Thanks."

"You know that's not what I meant," I said. "I've been here often enough to know the Tuesday afternoon schedule."

She pushed her chair back and stood. The tone of my voice was telling her plenty.

"All right," she said. She spoke slowly, half curious, half concerned. "What do you mean?"

It was strange. Being angry had taken all of

my shyness out of me. I was able to speak directly to her, without staring at the floor.

"What do I mean? For starters, Michah's not the first kid to have a seizure here."

"How do you know—"

"And he isn't the second kid to have a seizure here, either. Isn't he the fourth kid in four months to get sent to the hospital?"

"But—"

"Micah and his mother came to our game on Sunday afternoon. It was my first chance to speak to him since the hospital. He told me about three of his friends. Maybe you remember them. Nathan. Drew. Jamie. All of them had seizures. Right?"

"Yes, but—"

"And all of them have been told not to return to New Hope. Any reason?"

She took a deep breath and blinked a couple of times. "Insurance," she said. "It's difficult for organizations like ours to get insurance against being sued. We can't afford the risk of keeping kids who have proven they are likely to have seizures."

"Interesting," I replied. "Very interesting. Almost as interesting as finding out all four of them have ADHD. Do you think that's a coincidence?"

"ADHD?" Samantha blinked a few times again. "I don't understand."

"Attention deficit hyperactivity disorder. You know, a medical condition that some kids have. It makes them hyperactive, and they can't pay attention to anything for long. I find it strange that someone in your position pretends not to know what it is."

She blinked more. "I'm not pretending."

But she was pretending. I'd already made some phone calls. I'd already visited the mothers of Nathan and Rashawn and Jamie. Because of that, I knew Samantha was lying.

Her constant blinking seemed odd. I wondered if I could guess what it meant.

"And you don't know why Ben was kidnapped?" I asked.

"He just happened to be in the wrong place at the wrong time," she said. "It's not like someone was looking for him specifically."

This time, I expected her to blink. Which she did.

"If you want to lie to people," I said, "you should learn to be a better actress. You give yourself away by blinking. You can't look me in the eyes when you lie."

"You are rude. Please leave."

"I might be rude. But I do know Ben is in danger. In fact, I know you're supposed to keep your mouth shut about something or he'll get seriously hurt."

Her mouth dropped. "You can't know that," she managed to say in a whisper.

"I overheard Earl Chadley threathen you. I know plenty more too. After Micah told me about Nathan and Rashawn and Jamie, I called each of their mothers. Not only did I find out that all of the boys have been diagnosed with ADHD, but I also found out every one in our group suffers from it. Almost like you went out and collected kids who have ADHD."

That, of course, explained why they were so crazy and wild during our visits here. If it hadn't been for the street hockey to tire them out, Riley and I would have gone equally crazy trying to work with them.

"I found out something else," I said. "Micah, Jamie, Nathan, and Rashwawn had been making great progress. Every one of their mothers was sad to see them out of the program because every one of their mothers said the boys were so much quieter at home after time at New Hope."

I took a breath. "What I don't know is the big secret you're hiding. And I want to know it. Now."

"Drop it, Tyler," she said. Her face was white now. She wasn't blinking. "Drop the questions. Drop your volunteer time here. Drop everything and pretend you never once called those mothers. Then go back to hockey and forget you ever heard of New Hope."

"Why?" I said. "Give me one good reason why."

"Because you look much nicer in a hockey uniform than you would in a coffin."

Fifteen

Mr. Cranky Pants," Riley said to me as we walked away from the New Hope building toward my Jeep. "What's the matter? Did Sam turn you down for Normandale Student Night?"

Two hours had passed since my conversation with Samantha. Riley and I were both dripping sweat after a long run with the kids. I carried my gym bag in one hand, my Jeep keys in the other.

"I didn't ask her," I said.

"You spent enough time in her office when we got here," he said. "How could you not have asked her?"

Riley carried his own gym bag over his shoulders.

"You want to hear something crazy?" I asked.

We were almost at the Jeep.

"Sure."

I waited until we were both inside. Riley threw his gym bag on the floor at his feet. I put the key in the ignition. We both pulled our seat belts on.

I didn't start driving, though. Instead, I told Riley about the weird things I had discovered with my phone calls. An entire group of kids with ADHD. Four kids with seizures in four months. The mothers unhappy that the kids weren't allowed to come back to New Hope.

"Well no kidding," Riley said with his usual smart-aleck grin. "Sometimes ADHD kids use medication. So if your kid came home happy and tired and quiet, wouldn't you want him to stay in the program?"

Program.

That word kept going through my mind as Riley dug through the gym bag for his water bottle. He found it and offered it to me.

"Kool-Aid?" he asked. "I took some more from their snack tray while they weren't looking."

"Sure," I said. I gulped down some Kool-Aid and handed it back to him.

Program. Drugs.

I remembered the kidnapping van. It had been stolen from a pharmaceutical company. I remembered how it bugged me that the van had clean sides but a dirty back end.

Program. Drugs. Pharmaceutical company. What could it mean?

Riley almost had the water bottle to his mouth when I grabbed it from his hands.

"Hey! I'm willing to share! You don't have to be a jerk about it."

"Riley," I said. "You're allergic to a lot of things, right?"

"So?"

"I'm not. Which means I can handle a lot of things that you can't."

"So? What's your point? I'm thirsty. I'm not allergic to Kool-Aid, and I'm the one who got it for us. I deserve a drink as much as you do."

"No problem," I said. "Just answer me a couple of questions. When was the last time you had some of their Kool-Aid?"

He thought about it for a second. "Not the last time here. Micah had a seizure and I didn't get a chance to fill the bottle. So it was the time before."

"Exactly."

He nodded.

"Here's my other question," I continued. "When was the practice where you went blind for an hour?"

It took him much less time to answer this question. "Last time I had their Kool-Aid."

I remembered how my legs felt like wooden sticks. I hadn't gone blind like him, but I hadn't been my normal self either.

His eyes dropped to the water bottle in my hands. He repeated himself. "Kool-Aid! Are you trying to tell me . . ."

I offered him the water bottle. "Still want to share?"

He shook his head no.

Sixteen

The Kool-Aid," I said. "And I wonder if that also answers a lot of other things."

When I settled into the corner chair of Coach Fink's office on Wednesday morning, he didn't waste any time getting to the point.

"Tyler," he said, "on Sunday afternoon, with ten minutes left in the game, you had a chance to score the goal to put away the Thunderbirds. Remember?"

I nodded yes. I did remember. It would have almost been better if I hadn't even had the chance in the first place.

"And you couldn't have made it easier on the goalie if you had picked up the puck and handed it to him. Remember?"

I nodded yes again. I was highly aware of my gym bag at my feet. Whatever might happen during the next ten minutes of discussion, I had a question of my own.

"I know why," he said. "I know exactly why you didn't bury the puck. You had already scored a goal. You thought one was enough and you didn't want more."

"Well . . ." I said. He was probably close to the truth, but I didn't want to admit it.

"Tyler," he added, "you cause me as much grief as any player I have ever coached."

I thought back over the three years I had been in junior hockey, two under Fink as coach. I hadn't once missed curfew. I hadn't once yelled at him. In fact, I hadn't even been late for a single practice.

I mentioned all of this as I defended myself.

"I almost wish you would give me that kind of grief," Coach said. "At least I'd know what to do about it. I could bench you. Or I could fine you $3 in the team's Kangaroo Court. But what's it going to take to get you to play good hockey?"

His face showed concern. I think that made it worse. He wasn't mad. He wasn't disappointed. He was, if anything, sad to be needing to talk to me.

"You see," he went on, "you're big enough, you're talented enough. You can shoot." He winced, no doubt remembering how I had hit

Coach Talafous below the belt buckle during one practice. "Yup, you can shoot. But only in practice, not games. Same with your skating and stickhandling."

He paused and stared at me. "So what stops you from playing good hockey in game situations? You're not afraid to go into the corners and dig the puck out. When people push you around, you don't back away. We've kept you on the team this long because we keep hoping some day you'll break through and play the way you can. I half think you're just happy to be wearing the team jacket. But you don't want to face any pressure."

I let out a deep breath. "You're going to cut my game time, aren't you?"

He slammed his fist on his desk. He half stood. He yelled down on me. "Listen to your tone of voice! You don't even care!"

"That's not true," I said, "But—"

"Don't tell me you care! Look at you! Sitting there like we were discussing the weather. You're accepting whatever happens! Like if I benched you from the team after two years, it's no big deal!"

He pounded his fist again. "Where's your fire, Watson? What's it going to take to get you to do more than wear the team jacket?"

He repeated himself, spitting the words at me. "Where is your inner fire?"

Coach Fink sat back down and found his breath. He stared at me until I looked away. When he spoke again, he had himself under control.

"Do you think it was an accident that I paired you with Riley Judd? Sure I wanted you to help make him a team player. I didn't lie about that. But I was also hoping some of his fire would rub off on you. I was hoping you'd get mad enough and jealous enough of someone like him to actually play the way I know you can."

He snorted. "Hmmph. It's more like you managed to tie him to the same piano you choose to keep dragging around on the ice during hockey games. "

Coach Fink got up and started pacing around the office. He spoke more to himself than to me. "I've got Riley Judd, a million-dollar player who's starting to play like a ten-dollar player. And I've got you, a ten-dollar player who doesn't know he can play more like that million-dollar player. Maybe my mother was right; I should have coached pro wrestling."

He continued to shake his head and

grumble beneath his breath as he paced.

"I don't want to get cut," I said to his back.

He whirled and glared at me.

"What's that?"

"I don't want to get cut."

He moved directly in front of me, crossed his arms, and stared down at me. This was a new side of Coach Fink I had never seen before; even when he was frustrated with the whole team he got his point across with needing to scream and yell.

"I can't quite hear you, Watson."

"I don't want to get cut." I kept my voice even.

"Louder. You sound like a ballerina."

"I don't want to get cut."

"Shout it!"

I stood and stared right back into his eyes. "I am not going to play your dumb army-sergeant game. I will not shout like this is some kind of pep rally. But I will tell you this again. I want to play."

He grinned. "Finally. I see some fire in your eyes. You've got two more weeks, Watson. Show that fire on the ice, and you'll keep your ice time."

I did not grin in return. My teeth remained gritted.

"We have a light jog and stretch in fifteen minutes," he said. "You'd better get moving. And tonight, play hard."

I did not move.

He arched his eyebrows in surprise. "Yes, Tyler? Anything else?"

"Coach," I said. "It's about the piano you blamed me for tying to Riley Judd."

"This ought to be interesting," Coach Fink said.

"You know how sometimes players are tested for drugs?"

His face grew dark. "Drugs? Is Riley Judd into drugs?"

"Nothing like that," I said quickly. "I'm just hoping you know which doctor to call for drug testing."

"What exactly do you want to test?" he asked. He was frowning.

"This," I said. I leaned forward and pulled a water bottle out of my gym bag. "It looks and tastes like Kool-Aid, but I think it's a little stronger than the regular stuff."

Seventeen

A cut requiring five stitches definitely hurts. But it didn't hurt near as much as the smirk on Coach Fink's face.

"Yup, five stitches, Coach," Stephanie, our Certified Athletic Trainer said again, "maybe six. That flying puck cut him good. I don't think we can get by with just steri-strips."

Less than a minute earlier, I had been standing in front of the St. Paul Lakers' net, hoping to deflect a puck in for a goal. Instead, when our defenseman Andy Kautza had fired the slap shot from the point, the puck had ticked off the stick of a Lakers forward as he tried to block the puck. It had changed direction too quickly for me to duck and had nicked the edge of my jaw, sending me to the ice and stopping the play.

Now, I was sitting in the players' box. Stephanie had my head tilted backward to examine the bottom of my jaw. All I saw above me was her face. Along with Coach Fink's face and that know-it-all smirk.

I felt the warmth of blood as it trickled down my throat. Stephanie wiped it away with a gauze pad. On the ice, play continued. The third period had just started, and we were ahead of the Lakers, 5–3.

"Pretty deep cut, Steph," Coach agreed. Out came another smirk. "It's the perfect excuse for Tyler to leave the game. An injury sounds a lot better than just plain quitting."

"Unnunnh." I tried to say. It is difficult to speak when someone is holding your chin. I yanked my head away. More blood gushed down the skin of my throat. I pulled the gauze out of Stephanie's gloved hand and pressed it against the cut.

"Hurry up and just cover it," I said. "The stitches can wait."

"You're sure?" Coach Fink asked. "If you step back onto the ice, you're going to face pressure. Leave now, and you can walk around the stands with your Northern Lights jacket and look cool."

"Cover it quickly. I want to play."

Coach's smirk changed to a grin. "This morning's talk made a difference?"

"I want to play."

Coach nodded at Scotty. "Butterfly it. The boy wants to play."

Coach Fink left me and started his usual pacing behind the players. He shouted instructions to players jumping onto the ice as others stepped into the players' box. I could barely hear him above the crowd's constant noise.

Stephanie opened the first-aid kit and took out a bottle of adhesive and some bandage strips. She dabbed the adhesive over the cut, then used the bandage to pull the skin together tight enough to stop the bleeding until the period ended. Dr. Morrison, our team physician would stitch me up in our locker room later.

The good thing about getting cut in the heat of a game is that the pain doesn't hit until much later. I was ready to play. One shift later, Coach Fink sent me onto the ice.

Fine, I told myself. Coach thinks I'm a quitter? I'll score a goal and then make him eat the puck for breakfast.

Although the crowd was roaring its usual hometown support, I didn't look around the stands the way I usually did. I only had eyes for the puck.

Our shift began with a faceoff on the left side in the Lakers' end. The ref dropped the puck. Blake Sundeen, my center, managed to pull the puck back toward our defenseman on the Lakers' blue line.

Matt Johnson dodged their defensemen and broke hard for the net.

Instead of clogging the middle by breaking for the net myself, I drifted backward, finding open ice.

T.J. Lokken, on defense, faked a slap shot.

The Lakers' forward, rushing up, fell for the fake and dropped, sliding with his body stretched to block the shot. John easily pulled the puck to the side, and the Lakers' forward slid harmlessly by.

I yelled for the puck. I had my stick high in the air, ready for a slap shot.

Lokken snapped a pass toward me. It was coming so fast, I didn't have time to think about what I was doing. I just reacted, going into motion the way I had done hundreds of time in practice.

Timing it perfectly, I hammered my stick down at full speed just as the puck arrived. I redirected the puck, slapping it two feet off the ice at the net. It drove through a maze of players and found the mesh of the net behind the goalie.

The red light blinked as the goal judge behind the Plexiglas confirmed what I already knew.

I'd scored!

I was mad enough at Coach Fink that I didn't raise my arms in triumph, the usual reaction any time a player scores. Instead, I shrugged like hitting the prettiest slap shot of my life was just routine.

I'd scored so quickly that our line still had plenty of time left on this shift.

In my head, everything seemed quiet, like I had no thoughts. No worries. Just a calm peace and total concentration on the puck. Almost like when Sam and I had chased the kidnappers and they'd stepped out of their van armed with switchblades. Then, I'd only worried about how I was going to protect myself. Now, I only worried about the swoosh of my skates on the ice, the click of the puck on my stick. I liked the feeling, the tightness of determination that seemed to fill my stomach.

Sundeen lost the draw at center ice. Their center drew the puck back to their left defenseman, directly ahead of me. I charged ahead.

As expected, the defenseman passed around me to the Lakers' center who was cutting through the middle. I turned back, and jumped into full speed, chasing down the

Lakers' winger I was supposed to guard on my side of the ice. I followed the winger all the way to the top of our own faceoff circle, staying so close their center had no pass to my side and was forced to dump the puck behind our net.

Paul McGrath, as defenseman, picked up the puck. I stayed along the boards, giving him an outlet if he needed to pass to me.

The Lakers' forward stayed right beside me, guarding against a pass to me, just like I'd earlier guarded against a pass to him.

In theory, I was playing my position. No one could fault me for staying along the boards and tying up my man. It was the safe play. Nobody could blame me for any mistakes if I remained there.

I pushed off the boards, catching the Lakers' forward by surprise.

All right, Fink, I thought, you won't be able to say I don't try.

I busted for center ice, angling to keep myself open for a pass. I kept my stick down on the ice, giving the defenseman a target. I yelled for the puck.

He snapped it forward.

Out of the corner of my eye, I saw their defenseman. He'd moved up to body check me, hoping I'd have my head down as I tried to receive the long pass.

At the last second, I hit the brakes so hard that my skates skidded across the top of the ice. I braced for the hit, let the defenseman bounce off me, and then scrambled for the puck.

No thoughts cluttered my mind except to pump my legs as hard as I could. I chipped the puck ahead, sprinted to go wide around the remaining defenseman.

He slashed his stick down across my arm, trying to knock the puck loose. I didn't feel any pain; I felt detached from anything but the single thought of getting the puck to the net.

Clear of the final defenseman, I cut back to the center of the ice. There wasn't much time left as I reached the net. Without thinking, I made a fake to the left, drew the puck back in near my skates, flipped it to my backhand side, pulled it out of reach of the goalie, and banged it into the net.

The crowd went berserk.

I didn't. I skated back to the bench as if scoring two goals in one shift was no big deal.

Coach Fink thumped me on the back as I stepped into the players' bench.

"Great goals!" he shouted. "I knew you could do it!"

"Hmmph," I said.

I scored my third goal five minutes later, snapping a wristshot into the top left corner of the net from the top of the faceoff circle.

At the end of the game, two things happened.

Coach Fink told me to expect to play on the second line next game. And he sent me to the back room to get my face fixed up.

Stephanie was right. The cut took five stitches.

Eighteen

Driving my Jeep, I was daydreaming about my hat trick* the night before. Because it was a Thursday afternoon, Riley was beside me on our way to New Hope. We had hockey sticks for the kids in the far back portion of the Jeep, our gym bags in the backseat. We had made this trip twice a week so many times now that I didn't have to concentrate much to get us there.

As usual, just after exiting 35W, I swung into the right hand turn lane to go east on Lake Street. One block ahead, the light was green. I signaled for the turn, and slowed down for the corner at Second Avenue. Although it was green for me, a pedestrian stepped onto the crosswalk in front of the Jeep, and I had to slam on my brakes.

That took me out of my daydream in a big hurry.

"What an idiot!" Riley said. "Honk your horn."

"No sense," I said. "I've already stopped."

At the front of our hood, the man turned to face us. He had one hand in his pocket. There was something too familiar about his face.

Then I remembered! The walrus mustache!

He was one of the kidnappers who had taken Ben. He was one of the two men who had pulled a switchblade on me.

He grinned at the shock that must have shown on my face.

He stayed in front of the Jeep. Cars behind us began to honk.

I was too stunned to do anything. Besides, there was no place for me to go unless I ran him over.

He grinned more and motioned with his free arm like he wanted me to roll down my window. He pulled his other hand from his pocket and flashed us a switchblade.

"He's the guy!" I told Riley. "One of the kidnappers from the van!"

Riley didn't have a chance to reply. The rear passenger door clicked open.

We had been so busy staring at the guy in front of us that we hadn't noticed another man step off the sidewalk. Before I could react, the second man slid into the rear passenger seat, pushing the gym bags onto the floor.

"Boys," he said, "nice day isn't it?"

Riley spun around. "Get out of—"

"Shut your mouth, kid," the guy said with a sneer. "I've got a gun on the other side of this seat and it's aimed at you."

The other man walked around the side of the Jeep toward the rear door on my side.

"If you hit the gas, kid," the guy in the backseat said, "I pull the trigger on your friend."

The light was still green, that was how fast this had happened. Cars behind us kept honking for me to complete my right turn through the intersection. To them, it must have looked like I'd stopped to pick up a couple of friends. Despite the honking, I forced myself to wait until the second man got into the backseat directly behind me. He slammed the door shut.

He laughed.

"Thanks for stopping," he said. "Looks like a great day for a drive."

I was tempted to drop the Jeep into reverse and slam backward into the car behind me. A car accident would get these two out of the Jeep.

I lifted my hand to the gearshift.

"Don't try anything stupid," the guy behind me said. He spoke in a cheerful tone, as if we were old friends.

I hesitated. The honking grew louder.

"And while people are trying to stop your bleeding, Ron and me will make another getaway. Understand?"

I eased the Jeep forward.

"That's better," he said. "You just keep taking directions, and you'll be just fine."

"This is nuts," Riley said. "You can't do this to us."

"We've got a switchblade and a gun," the second guy said. "I think we can do whatever we want."

Fifteen minutes later, we drove around the back of an abandoned one-story warehouse near the Mississippi River and stopped. They forced us out of the jeep at gun point and took us to the trunk of a huge, rusty, old baby-blue Cadillac.

The one named Ron banged on the top of the trunk.

"We're opening it up!" he shouted. "And we've still got the gun. Don't do anything stupid!"

Who was he talking to?

Ron fumbled with a set of keys and clicked open the lock of the trunk. The door swung upward, throwing dust in our faces. Coughing and a dirty face greeted us.

Samantha?

"Get in and make yourselves comfy," he told us. "The three of you can have a little tea party in there while we take you for a nice long drive."

"P. S.," he said with an evil grin. "If you start screaming for help, Frankie here will fire a couple of rounds through the backseat into the trunk. And trust me, you won't have much room to dodge bullets."

Nineteen

Sam?" I asked in the darkness of the closed trunk. A tire jack pressed against my ribs. My elbows were folded below me. I was facing backward, between Samantha and Riley. Both of them were on their sides, almost curled against me. It was not my idea of a little tea party.

The Cadillac bounced over bumps in the warehouse parking lot. I couldn't see where we were going, but I could see where we had been. A tiny peephole had rusted through the trunk, giving me a small circular view of the world the Cadillac left behind.

"I'm okay," she said. "Just thirsty. The jerks grabbed me about three hours ago. Just as I was leaving my apartment."

"But why?" Riley said.

Sam didn't say anything to his question.

"The drug-testing program," I said. "Beckstead Pharmaceuticals."

"How did you know that?" Samantha gasped.

"Just guessing." Her brother had been kidnapped in a pharmaceuticals' van with a dirty license plate. Except the sides of the van had been shiny clean, as if someone had just thrown mud on the back to cover the plates— not like the van had driven through mud. So maybe the company had just said it was stolen.

"Ouch," Riley said as we hit a big bump. "Hey, Tyler, is that who put drugs in the Kool-Aid?"

"You guessed that too!" Samantha said with another gasp. "But how?"

I wished we were having this conversation in a police station. Or in Coach Fink's office. Anywhere but in the locked trunk of a Cadillac with two lunatics taking us for a long drive.

"You know I overheard the director threaten you with Ben's safety. That started me wondering," I told Samantha. Actually, I told it to her feet, which were pressed into my shoulders.

"Am I right?" I asked.

She took so long to answer, I began to

wonder if she had even heard me.

The Cadillac moved steadily through traffic. The peephole showed me plenty of cars behind us. An old lady in a Volkswagen Beetle. A family in a van. A business man in another Cadillac—much newer than this one—tapping his fingers impatiently on the steering wheel as he waited behind us for a light to change. All of these people in their own little worlds, and they had no idea there were three of us stuffed into the trunk of the Cadillac right in front of them. It made me want to scream in frustration. But I didn't want to give the lunatics inside the Cadillac a reason to start firing bullets through the backseat into the trunk.

"Yes, you're right, Tyler," Samantha finally said. "But I'm not sure it does us much good at this point."

She explained. It took some doing, over the rumblings of exhaust pipes and through the stops and starts of the Cadillac as it moved through traffic. What she told us added to what I had already managed to guess.

The New Hope kids were chosen to belong to the program if they came from single-mother homes and if they had been diagnosed with Attention Deficit Hyperactivity Disorder.

Samantha said that most ADHD kids were

extremely bright. But because of various medical reasons, they tended to be hyperactive and had difficulty concentrating on one thing for any length of time. Sometimes, ADHD kids take medication, and it helps them focus.

Single mothers with ADHD kids were usually glad to have someone help them. Not only that, these mothers often received payment for letting their kids belong. They were told that the money was part of the New Hope approach to helping kids in all areas of life. New Hope wanted the kids to get better food and clothing at home. Because of the extra help and because of the money, the mothers didn't ask questions about the program. Especially since their kids came home calm after time in New Hope.

The reason they were less hyperactive, of course, was the Kool-Aid. Or, rather, because of what was in the Kool-Aid.

The kids, as I had guessed, were part of an experimental program, run by a Minnesota company called Beckstead Pharmaceuticals. Although there was medication already available for ADHD kids, Beckstead wanted to find faster-acting medication.

Samantha said that any pharmaceutical company that discovered a better way to treat

ADHD could make up to $50 million in profit in the first year alone.

New medications, however, have to be tested for years before the government approves them. Beckstead was in financial trouble and needed to get their new drug on the market much sooner. They didn't want to waste time having the government test drugs that might not work. Instead, they wanted to deliver something that would pass all tests as soon as possible.

That's where New Hope came in. The kids came from backgrounds where parents would be unlikely to ask questions, where parents would not have the education or money to file lawsuits, even if they did suspect something was wrong. In fact, if a kid had a seizure, he wasn't allowed back to the program, just in case the parents started comparing stories and realizing how unusual it was for so many kids to have seizures.

They resulted from the experimental drugs in the Kool-Aid. Most of the kids were fine with it—Beckstead Pharmaceuticals did want a safe drug. But not everyone reacted the same way to the drug. Including Riley. Because of his allergies, he'd gone blind for nearly an hour when all it had done to me was make me tired and stiff.

To run the experiments, the kids were watched and tested before and after their snack break. Some got Kool-Aid with the drug. Some got Kool-Aid without it. Those who did, however, usually calmed down. Riley and I had never noticed a huge difference in their behavior because we kept them running around playing street hockey.

Samantha, however, saw them every day in several settings and did see differences.

She also knew about the number of seizures.

She knew the kids all had ADHD, except for Ben, who wasn't really part of the program.

She had seen the blood tests given to some of the kids and heard the excuses—that they were being tested for polio and other diseases that sometimes hit kids in poor neighborhoods.

She had begun to ask questions. But she had asked the wrong person, Earl Chadley, who was the interim director at New Hope, not knowing he received tens of thousands of dollars in bribes to allow the ADHD experiment to continue. He was not part of the church staff and had even lied on his resume to get the temporary position.

At that point, the two thugs in the front seat were brought in by Beckstead

Pharmaceuticals. They had kidnapped Ben intending to scare Sam into silence before releasing Ben back to her.

Because of me, however, the kidnapping had failed. Sam had asked a few more questions, which had led to the conversation I had overheard the afternoon I broke a window with my slap shot.

Even so, nothing would have happened. Samantha was scared enough to keep her mouth shut, and the program might have continued.

Except for one thing. Me and my big mouth. Me and my big mouth the afternoon I had marched into her office and demanded that she explain some things.

"A voice-activated tape recorder?" Riley asked as Sam told us how they had discovered my interest in the Kool-Aid. "In your office, Sam?"

We had been in traffic for nearly twenty minutes. My body ached from bouncing around inside the trunk. My muscles felt cramped, my nose full of dirt. My skin was itchy too. I wondered if the trunk had bugs in it.

"That's what Ron and Frankie, our two friends in the front seat, told me," Sam said. "A voice-activated tape recorder. When you think of all they have at stake, it shouldn't be a surprise. They needed to know everything that was going on around New Hope. When Tyler barged into my office with all his questions, it didn't take them long to realize they needed to stop him too."

"But why me?" Riley asked. "I didn't ask any questions."

"You were at New Hope with Tyler," she said. "They didn't know if you knew anything. And for all they had at stake, they weren't going to take any chances."

"They won't get away with this," I said. "I already gave some of the Kool-Aid to Coach Fink. The tests will show something was in there. And Coach Fink knows the Kool-Aid came from New Hope."

"That's right!" Riley's muffled voice said. "Kidnapping us won't help keep this a secret! Once we explain that to Ron and Frankie, they'll have to let us go. Otherwise, they'll be in even bigger trouble. I mean, it's one thing to throw a drug or two into some Kool-Aid. It's another to haul people away in a beat-up old car."

"Wrong," Samantha said.

The way she said it sent chills down my hunched back. She spoke as if she had no hope.

"Look," she said. "How do you think I know so much about all of this? Louie and Ron had a lot of fun telling me. They also told me about your Kool-Aid test. Do you think once they knew you were asking questions that they would take any chances at all?"

"Coach Fink took the water bottle from my hand," I said stubbornly. "And he's not part of this. He will get it tested."

"Sure he will," she said. "But it won't be the Kool-Aid they used on the kids. Beckstead Pharmaceuticals has connections everywhere. And they've been watching everything you do. They knew the Kool-Aid was going to a lab to be tested. They switched the samples."

"Impossible!" I said.

"Impossible? Your team doctor is a man named Morrison, right?"

"Right," I said, suddenly feeling even worse, if that was possible.

"Just this afternoon Ron and Frankie bragged about how they had broken into Doctor Morrison's office and made it look like a robbery. Only their real reason was to switch Kool-Aid samples. When the tests come back, they will show nothing unusual."

"Great," I said. I kept looking out the peephole of the trunk. It might not do me any good to know where we were going, but I was doing my best to figure it out.

"It gets worse," she said.

"Worse?" Riley said. "I can hardly wait to hear this."

"Ron and Frankie told me that Beckstead is ending the program. They're going to stop testing kids at New Hope and look for another place to start testing kids. We came too close to finding the answers."

"You sure know a lot," I grumbled.

"That's the worst news of all," Samantha said. "They don't care what we know."

"Your point?" Riley asked.

"Did they hide their faces from you?" she asked him in return. "Are they worried you'll ever have a chance to testify against them in court?"

"No," he said. His voice was small. He knew what she meant.

"You see," Samantha said, "if they stop running the program at New Hope and if there is no drugged Kool-Aid around to show it was used in an experiment, nobody can ever prove that testing was done."

"Nobody except for us," I said. I winced as the Cadillac bounced through a pothole.

"Exactly," she told us. "There was a reason they were happy to tell me everything. They know we won't have a chance to let anyone else know. I mean, there's a reason we're in such a junker."

I didn't dare ask.

"If the car was newer," Samantha continued, "it would cost them that much more when they drive it into Lake Mille Lacs. Which is their way of making sure we keep our mouths shut forever."

Twenty

Well over an hour later we were still in the trunk. Through my peephole, I had watched the late afternoon light become dusk, then darkness. Since I had not been able to see the sun behind us, I knew we were driving toward the sun, which meant we were headed west, toward Lake Mille Lacs. And a real long good-bye.

For most of that time, we had traveled on a highway, with the tires whining at high speeds on the pavement. There wasn't much traffic on this highway. As evening approached, I had seen only occasional headlights behind us.

The Cadillac began to slow down.

"This isn't good, is it?" Riley said. "We've got to do something before they reach the lake."

I'd been thinking the same thing. But what?

We couldn't kick the trunk open. If we tried, they would hear the noise, and they would be right there with the .45 Magnum and the knife. While I had been able to work my arms loose from under my body and I had fiddled with the trunk lock almost in front of my face, there seemed to be no way for me to open it. And again, they had the gun and switchblade.

Unfortunately, Riley was right. If the Cadillac was slowing down, it meant we were that much closer to the moment they would drive this car off a cliff.

I tried to remember what I knew about Minnesota geography when I was applying for my fishing license and looking for good lakes within a few hours of the metro area. Lake Mille Lacs was around eighty miles from Minneapolis. If we had averaged 55 miles an hour since getting out of the city, it meant we were close. Too close.

The Cadillac stopped.

"Relax, guys," I said. "Traffic light. We're in some town." Through the peephole, I could see cars pulling up behind us. The cars were lit by street lights.

What town? I wondered.

I got my answer at the next traffic light. Although I couldn't see much through the peephole, by pressing my head as close as possible, I was able to read some signs. I saw a motel. The Onamia Motel.

I passed the information on to Riley and Samantha.

"Onamia?" Samantha said. "That's almost at the lake. I remember some cabins towns north of here."

"With docks you can drive on?" Riley asked.

"With docks," she said quietly.

Riley didn't say anything until the next traffic light. "Well, Tyler," he announced, trying to keep his voice cheerful, "at least I won't have to lie awake at night and worry if I'll go blind or if my heart will stop beating."

"And I won't have to worry about losing my spot on the Northern Lights game roster," I said.

The Cadillac rumbled as it idled at the traffic light.

"Probably too late," Riley said, "but I just thought of something. When you die, it's one thing or the other."

"Do we have to talk about dying?" Samantha said. "I'm scared enough."

"Unless we find a way to pop the trunk open when this car hits the lake . . ."

"Thanks, Riley," I said. "I was doing my best to ignore that."

"That's what I mean," he said. "I've always

ignored the fact I would die. And that either God is really there, or he isn't. I'd never thought of that before. It's one or the other. And I guess I should spend some time thinking about it to at least make up my mind about what I believe before I die."

I kept my eye at the peephole. If this was the last I would see of the world, I was going to be as greedy as possible and see as much as I could.

"Are you talking about God because you're scared?" I asked.

"Of course I'm not scared," he said sarcastically, "I look forward to drowning in a Cadillac. Especially an old ugly one."

I saw a car a block away. At first, I didn't want to dare believe what I saw. When it passed beneath the next street light, I saw the light bubble on top. It was a Highway Patrol car.

I nearly shouted the good news to Riley and Samantha. Until I realized it wasn't good news. The troopers were right there, pulling up behind us, but there was no way we could get their attention.

I wanted to bang my head on the floor of the trunk. It would pop my stitches open, but who cared. This was like being on a raft in the middle of the ocean and watching search planes in the distance as they flew right by without seeing you.

The police car eased up closer. For a moment, I saw both officers' faces in the windshield. The driver was sipping from a coffee cup. The other had a half-eaten donut in his hand. Then the police car pulled up so close to the Cadillac's bumper that all I saw was the shiny silver grill.

"But a person might die any day, right?" Riley was saying. "Like if you stepped in front of a bus. Or a drunk driver hit you. Or . . ."

"Riley! Please!" Samantha said.

"I'm sorry," Riley said. "It's just that—"

"Enough already," she told him. "I thought jocks didn't think. You're supposed to be stupid."

I knew I felt stupid. There was a police car right behind us. I couldn't think of a single thing to do to get their attention. I wondered if yelling would get the attention of the cops.

Probably not. If they were talking with the windows closed, they wouldn't hear us. And Ron and Frankie in the front would definitely hear.

On the other hand, if we were going to die anyway, what would we have to lose by shouting?

I lifted my head to get a good lungful of air, and my face tangled on some electrical wiring.

"All right then," Riley said. "I'll change the subject. How's this? Tyler wants to invite you to the Normandale Student Night, but he's too afraid. So I'll ask for him. Would you go with him?"

I kicked Riley. He grunted.

"Well—" Samantha said.

"Of course, you're going to say yes," I said. "We're about to die. You're not going to hurt my feelings by turning me down to a activity we'll never get to."

It made me mad that Riley had embarrassed me. I slapped at the stupid wires. I sucked some air in again and almost began to yell, even knowing how useless it would be.

Then I realized what the wires meant. Now I might be able to get the attention of the police in the car behind us.

I grabbed the wires and yanked as hard as I could.

Twenty-One

The Cadillac took off slowly when the traffic light turned green. One minute later—I was counting the seconds heartbeat by heartbeat—I saw the sweetest sight I'd ever seen.

Red and blue flashing lights filled the tiny circle of my peephole as the police car closed the gap and tried to pull us over. I told Riley and Samantha what was happening.

"Cops!" Riley said. "They're stopping this car?"

"I just hope Ron and Frankie don't try to outrun them," I answered.

"But—"

I interrupted Riley. "Here's the deal. As soon as this car is stopped and the police get out of their car, start yelling and screaming and kicking the trunk lid."

"They'll shoot us if we make noise," Riley said. "Remember?"

"With the cops right there? Not a chance. Kidnapping is one thing. But are they going to murder us with the cops watching?"

We felt the Cadillac swerve as Ron and Frankie decided to pull over. And why not? Ron and Frankie probably didn't know about the rust hole that I was able to peek through. I was willing to bet they figured Riley and Samantha and I had no idea they were stopping for the officers. If we didn't know it was officers, we sure wouldn't be brave enough to make noise. If we didn't make noise, the officers would have no reason to look in the trunk. So why risk everything by trying to outrun the police?

The Cadillac settled on its springs as it stopped.

I heard the crunching of tire on rocks as the police car stopped behind the Cadillac. Again, all I could see through the peephole was the shiny silver grill.

The police car doors opened and slammed shut.

Footsteps approached the Cadillac.

It was now or never.

"Guys," I said, "start pounding and screaming."

We did. We hollered and bellowed and kicked at the trunk lid. Dirt fell into my face and nostrils, and I choked as it coated the inside of my throat.

No bullets tore through the backseat at our noise. No screeching of tires as the Cadillac took off.

We found out later that as soon as the officers heard the screaming and thumping, they pulled their guns and held them on the surprised Ron and Frankie.

We kept hollering and screaming and kicking until the trunk popped open and a flashlight blinded us.

"Teenagers!" a deep voice said with great surprise. "Three of them."

He clicked the flashlight off. We were able to see his tall silhouette above us, the wide brim of his hat clearly outlined against the street lights.

"Come on out," he said. "You'll be fine now. Just tell us what this is all about."

We climbed into the glare of headlights and flashing lights. Louie and Ron were braced against the side of the Cadillac. The other State Patrol officer guarded them with his revolver.

"Tell you what this is about?" I repeated. I drew a deep breath. "Sir, I would be happy to do just that."

◆

Within ten minutes, the state troopers had Ron and Frankie handcuffed and in the backseat of the police cruiser.

The larger of the two troopers stood outside the cruiser, speaking into the hand-held mike of the police radio.

The shorter one joined me and Riley and Samantha.

"We've called for a back-up cruiser. The boys will take you to the station. We'll need to file a report. Don't be surprised if it takes a few hours. Are you okay with that?"

Riley and I gave each other high fives. I winced at the pain of my palms slapping on his.

"We're okay with that," Riley said.

The officer pushed back the brim of his hat and surveyed us with his hands on his hips.

"Lucky for you that the tail lights on this old Cadillac burned out," he said. "Otherwise we would never have pulled it over."

"Um, I'm not sure it was luck," I said.

"What do you mean, son?"

I opened my hands and looked down at my palms. Both were cut where the wire had sliced through the skin when I yanked on the electrical wires.

"Well sir, last summer I was pretty mad at

the police because I got a ticket when a fuse on my Jeep went out and my brake lights didn't work. But if I hadn't gotten that ticket, I would never have thought of the idea."

I showed him my hands. "I was hoping if I disconnected the wires to their tail lights, you would do the same to them."

The trooper laughed. "Impressive son, mighty impressive."

Another Highway Patrol car arrived, ending our conversation.

Riley and Samantha and I walked over and climbed into the backseat of the second cruiser. I went first, then Samantha, then Riley.

The officer in the front seat hadn't even taken the car out of park, when Samantha leaned her face close to my ear.

"Tyler Watson," she whispered. "The answer is yes."

"Pardon me?"

"The Normandale Student Night," she said. "The answer is yes. Unless Riley lied and got my hopes up for nothing."

"Friday night," I said quickly, before she could change her mind. "I'll pick you up at seven."

Twenty-Two

How was your night out at Normandale?" Riley asked as he saw me in the lobby of the ice arena. "Did you and Samantha smooch when you drove her home?"

"Very funny," I said. "Are you ready for the Minnesota Owls?"

"Changing the subject are we?"

"She'll be in the stands tonight," I said. "Is that enough of an answer?"

"Sure." Riley grinned. He waved at a couple of the guys heading toward the dressing room for the usual pre-game warm-up.

"It's been a wild week, hasn't it?" he said, as we joined the guys.

"Yup." The cuts sliced into my palm were nearly healed. We had endured dozens of phone calls for newspaper interviews. We had faced police, lawyers, and television cameras. Most of it had happened because Ron and Frankie had decided to testify against Beckstead Pharmaceuticals in exchange for reduced jail sentences. Without their testimony to match ours, it would have been hard to prove that the ADHD kids had been used in an experimental program. Now, because of upcoming lawsuits against the company, it looked like every one of the kids involved in the program would get a hundred thousand dollars, enough to help their families and put them through college when they were older.

Even Riley and I had gotten some reward money. Not much, just enough to buy in-line skates and hockey equipment for every kid in our New Hope group. It sure had been fun watching them try out their new skates when we played street hockey with them.

Yes, it had been a wild week. But that was the past. This was now. I had a MJHL hockey game to worry about. Coach Fink had moved me to the second line, and I wanted to stay there.

"I've got a question for you," I said as we walked past Coach Fink's office. He was sitting behind his desk. He gave us a friendly wave through the open door.

"Fire away," Riley said.

"Now that you're back to your usual one or two goals a game, what do you think of just before you score a goal?"

"Huh?"

"You've got the puck on your stick, a chance to score. What do you think of in that moment?"

Riley stared at me and scratched his head. "Nothing, I guess," he finally said.

"Nothing?" His answer didn't surprise me.

Riley frowned in thought. "It's like I'm in a zone. Just me and the puck and the net. I don't hear anything. I don't feel anything. So the answer is that I don't think about anything."

"Do you worry about missing the net?" I asked. "Falling down? Making a mistake? Becoming a hero? Winning the scoring race?"

"Not when the puck is on my stick."

I nodded agreement. "One more thing. Over the last few weeks you were worried about going blind. It took your concentration away, didn't it? That's why you hit the slump, right?"

"I'm not worried about going blind anymore, if that's what you mean. I still think about the other stuff, like what happens when you die. And how amazing it is that we can see or breathe in the first place. And could our body parts be that detailed and specialized without a Designer? And have you ever wondered why so many people still believe in Jesus, even though he died two thousand years ago." He grinned. "Heavy duty philosophy, eh? Funny how being locked in a trunk can make you think."

I could learn from Riley. He never held back in hockey or anything else.

"Tell you what," I said, deciding that a person doesn't need to be invisible with what he believes. "Any time you want, let's talk about it."

"Not on the ice," he said, still grinning. "I'm through thinking and worrying out there. If you want the puck in the net, that's all you can have on your mind when the puck's on your stick."

"Thanks," I said. "You've said a lot I needed to hear." I gave him a grin and stepped into the familiar chatter and the familiar sweat and heat-liniment smell of the dressing room. Ducking as a pair of socks flew across the room at Mike Stone, one of our goalies, I found a place to sit.

As I dressed in my hockey equipment, I thought about what Riley had said. I also thought back to some of the other things that had happened in the last month or so.

I'd stepped out of the Jeep, armed with only

a hockey stick against Ron and Frankie with their switchblades. At the time, all I had been concentrating on was how to knock the knives from their hands. I hadn't worried about getting cut or about being a hero for Sam. My only thought had been on their switchblades and knocking them away.

When I'd fired a beauty of a slap shot into the corner boards and accidentally hit Coach Fink, my only thought had been on ripping the puck. Not on where it might go. Not on whether it would score.

When I'd stepped into another slap shot and broken the window at New Hope, again, my only thought had been on making contact with the ball. I'd been pure, fluid motion in perfect timing, with nothing in my head except the desire to smoke the shot.

The game against the St. Paul Lakers, I'd skated back onto the ice with steri-strips holding the skin on my jaw together. I'd been so mad at Coach Fink that all I wanted to do was skate hard and shoot hard. I hadn't worried about whether the shot missed the net, how the crowd would react, or if I'd be in the sports section of the newspaper the next day.

And in the trunk of the car, when I'd finally stopped worrying about what would happen when we went off the cliff and had concentrated on getting the cops' attention, my mind had found a way to solve the problem.

All of this was interesting to me. Real interesting.

Part of what made Riley Judd so good in hockey was that he concentrated on the puck. Nothing in his head got in the way.

Could I learn to do the same?

I hoped so.

I slipped my shin pads into my hockey socks, taped the shin pads tight and snugged the top of my socks with my garters. I stepped into my breezers, and put my skates on, leaving them unlaced. I put on my shoulder pads and my elbow pads.

My helmet was on the bench beside me. Along with my Northern Lights jersey.

All I needed to do was tie my skates, pull my belt tight on my hockey pants, get my sweater on, and strap my helmet into place.

I didn't, though.

I sat without moving for a couple more minutes, letting the chatter of the dressing room flow around me.

Maybe that was the key. I would concentrate on the task, not on the result. When I had the puck, I would try to get into the zone of nothingness where all that mattered was what I was doing in that very second.

Could I find that zone when I needed it?

Probably not every time. But I was willing to believe if I worked at it, I'd learn it better. And hockey would be more fun.

Someone slapped my shoulder. I broke out of my thoughts and looked up at Riley. He was already in his equipment, ready to step onto the ice for pre-game warm-up.

"What do ya say, Tyler?" he asked. "Gonna score a couple goals tonight with Samantha watching in the stands?"

"Tell you what, pal." I grabbed my sweater and pulled it over my head. "Don't be surprised when it happens."

Player Profile

#17

Name: Andy Kautza

Height: 6'2"

Weight: 200 pounds

Date of Birth: 04/04/84

Hometown: Merrill, WI

Position: Defence

School: Merrill High School

Favorite Children's Book: *Where the Red Fern Grows*

Words of Wisdom: Push yourself in all situations; strive to succeed.

Most Memorable Hockey Moment: Playing Junior Hockey

Player Profile

#18

Name: Louie Bruno III

Height: 5'8"

Weight: 195 pounds

Date of Birth: 12/03/84

Hometown: Atlanta, Georgia

Position: Forward

School: Hopkins High School

Favorite Children's Book: *The Stinky Cheese Man*

Words of Wisdom: Take school seriously

Most Memorable Hockey Moment: Playing at the Peewee Quebec Tournament

Player Profile

#19

Name: Jason Dobes

Height: 5'10"

Weight: 160 pounds

Date of Birth: 3/13/85

Hometown: Waterloo, IA

Position: Forward

School: Waterloo High School, IA

Favorite Children's Book: *Cat in the Hat*

Words of Wisdom: Stand firm for what you believe

Most Memorable Hockey Moment: Getting three points in the Iowa High School Tournament

Player Profile

#20

Name: Ryan Hampson

Height: 6'1"

Weight: 180 pounds

Date of Birth: 08/25/85

Hometown: Minnetonka, MN

Position: Defence

School: Minnetonka High School (Senior)

Favorite Children's Book: *The Hobbit*

Words of Wisdom: Try your best at everything

Most Memorable Hockey Moment: Playing in the Silver Stick PeeWee Finals in Michigan

Player Profile

#21

Name: Jon Jonasson
Height: 6'0"
Weight: 195 pounds
Date of Birth: 06/14/85
Hometown: Bloomington, MN
Position: Forward

School: Bloomington Kennedy High School
Favorite Children's Book: *Green Eggs & Ham*
Words of Wisdom: Reading will make you smarter
Most Memorable Hockey Moment: Watching Wayne Gretzky's last game

Player Profile

#23

Name: Shawn Hogan

Height: 6'0"

Weight: 180 pounds

Date of Birth: 06/14/85

Hometown:
Apple Valley, MN

Position: Forward

School: Apple Valley High School

Favorite Children's Book: *Green Eggs & Ham*

Words of Wisdom: Make smart choices …

Most Memorable Hockey Moment: My first goal in Junior Hockey – against the MN Owls

Player Profile

#24

Name: Brent Hanus

Height: 5'7"

Weight: 150 pounds

Date of Birth: 01/29/85

Hometown: Minnetonka, MN

Position: Forward

School: Minnetonka High School

Favorite Children's Book: *The Cat in the Hat*

Words of Wisdom: Always work your hardest in school -- if you don't, you'll regret it

Most Memorable Hockey Moment: My first high school hockey goal and being the leading scorer my Senior year in high school

Player Profile

#25

Name: Ryan Marshall

Height: 6'0"

Weight: 187 pounds

Date of Birth: 03/08/85

Hometown:
Inver Grove Heights, MN

Position: Forward

School: Simley High School

Favorite Children's Book: *The Missing Piece*

Words of Wisdom: Pay attention!

Most Memorable Hockey Moment: When I made Squirt in my second year of playing hockey ever! I worked really hard

#26

Name: Tim Hansen

Height: 5'10"

Weight: 150 pounds

Date of Birth: 11/16/84

Hometown:
New Hope, MN

Position: Defence

School: Cooper High School

Favorite Children's Book: *One Fish Two Fish, Red Fish, Blue Fish*

Words of Wisdom: Don't wait until the last minute to do your homework

Most Memorable Hockey Moment: Scoring two goals in my very first varsity high school hockey game

#27

Name: Dan Ohmann

Height: 6'0"

Weight: 175 pounds

Date of Birth: 8/15/85

Hometown:
Inver Grove Heights

Position:
Forward/Defence

School: Simley High School

Favorite Children's Book: *Clifford the Big Red Dog*

Words of Wisdom: Work to improve even the little things

Most Memorable Hockey Moment: Winning 2nd place in the MN State HS Tournament

#33

Name: Andy Singer

Height: 5'11"

Weight: 180 pounds

Date of Birth: 07/06/84

Hometown: Lakeville, MN

Position: Forward

School: Lakeville High School

Favorite Children's Book: *Green Eggs & Ham*

Words of Wisdom: Obey your parents

Most Memorable Hockey Moment: Playing in the Minnesota State High School Hockey Tournament at the Xcel Energy Center

#30

Name: Mike Stone

Height: 5'9"

Weight: 160 pounds

Date of Birth: 02/04/83

Hometown:
West Saint Paul

Position: Goalie

School: Henry Sibley High School

Favorite Children's Book: *When the Grinch Stole Christmas*

Words of Wisdom: Try new things even if they seem hard

Most Memorable Hockey Moment: Playing in the 2003 Junior Hockey National Tournament

#32

Name: Andrew Kent

Height: 5'9"

Weight: 175 pounds

Date of Birth: 04/21/84

Hometown:
Lakeville, MN

Position: Goalie

School: Lakeville High School

Favorite Children's Book: *Old Yeller*

Words of Wisdom: Don't do drugs

Most Memorable Hockey Moment: First game in net as a Northern Light

Player Profile

#35

Name: Kevin Johnson

Height: 5'11"

Weight: 175 pounds

Date of Birth: 01/06/85

Hometown: Wayzata, MN

Position: Goalie

School: Wayzata High School

Favorite Children's Book: *Bernstein Bears*

Words of Wisdom: Do your homework and it will pay off in class

Most Memorable Hockey Moment: Getting voted captain and MVP of my high school varsity team

Name: Eric Fink

Hometown: Sauk Rapids, MN

Position: Head Coach

School: Sauk Rapids High School

Favorite Children's Book: *Wait 'til Helen Comes*

Words of Wisdom: Follow your dreams

Most Memorable Hockey Moment: WILD upsetting Colorado Avalanche in game 7

Staff Profile

Name: Ross Smith

Hometown: Hopkins, MN

Position: President/General Manager

School: Chantilly High School, VA

Favorite Children's Book: *Cars and Trucks and Things that Go*

Words of Wisdom: Write down as much as you can so you will remember it in 20 years

Most Memorable Hockey Moment: The day we took over the South Suburban Steers

Staff Profile

Name: Stephanie Smith

Hometown: St. Louis, MO

Position: Strength and Condition Coach; Athletic Trainer

School: Ladue High School

Favorite Children's Book: *Nancy Drew & Hardy Boys series*

Words of Wisdom: Accept that there is a God and you're not Him.

Most Memorable Hockey Moment: Watching the 1980 Olympic team light the 2002 torch and then working the men's and women's hockey games in Salt Lake City.

Staff Profile

Assistant Coach: Gordie Hampson

Assistant Coach: Rob Talafous

Assistant Coach: Ryan Krmpotich

Team Physician: Dr. Grant Morrison

Board of Directors:

Mike Bachman
Ed & Maureen Krmpotich
Jim Mone
Tracy Patterson
Bill Penners
Rick & Nancy Subra
Anne Marie Urich
Wayne & Vicky Erickson
Ross & Stephanie Smith

Thank you to the following agencies for their support of our team:

North American Mission Board (SBC)
Minnesota Wisconsin Baptist Convention
Hockey Ministries International
Total Hockey Training

NORTHERN LIGHTS
INFORMATION:

Although this mystery story is completely
fiction, the Twin Cities Northern Lights team
does train and play their homes games at the
Bloomington Ice Garden. Several details in
the book, like names of people, teams, and
locations in Minnesota were added to make
the book more realistic, but this story is not
true. For the story behind the story, check
out the team's website:
www.northernlightshockey.com
Minnesota Junior Hockey League:
www.mnjhl.com

It's cool to stay in school!